DISNEY PIRATES JACK SPARROW

The Tale of Billy Turner and Other Stories

by Rob Kidd

Illustrated by Jean-Paul Orpinas

Based on the earlier life of the character, Jack Sparrow,
created for the theatrical motion picture,
"Pirates of the Caribbean: The Curse of the Black Pearl"
Screen Story by Ted Elliott & Terry Rossio and Stuart Beattie and Jay Wolpert,
Screenplay by Ted Elliott & Terry Rossio,
and characters created for the theatrical motion pictures
"Pirates of the Caribbean: Dead Man's Chest" and
"Pirates of the Caribbean: At World's End"
written by Ted Elliott and Terry Rossio

DISNEY PRESS

New York

For Domenica
—R.

For John Tucker
—Jean-Paul

Special thanks to
Rich Thomas, Ken Becker, and Liz Rudnick

Printed in the United States of America

First Edition
1 3 5 7 9 10 8 6 4 2

Library of Congress Catalog Card Number on file.

ISBN 978-1-4231-1803-9

DISNEYPIRATES.COM

The Tale of Billy Turner
and Other Stories

CHAPTER ONE

*T*he sea was empty.

This was the only conclusion that could be drawn by the people of the Isle of Man during one unusually hot, dry September during the first half of the eighteenth century. It had been almost a full year since they'd harvested a single adult cod or pollack, though the waters around the island were usually teeming with both.

Most people on the island chose not to

talk about the famine. The silence was brought about in part due to the superstitious belief that speaking of the tragedy would invite more disaster. But it also was an attempt to keep the dire situation off people's minds. It would seem that no one wanted to suffer the fate of Mister McGochen. The old man, driven mad by poverty and hunger, had sailed his failing boat into a warm July sunset and never returned.

Truth be told, however, some of the island's inhabitants *envied* Mister McGochen. To be free of the Isle would be a gift, even if sailing a rickety boat off into the vast reaches of forever was the only way to escape. After all, evidence of the famine was everywhere, not just in the sea. It had transformed the island into a bleak place. Without fish, there was nothing to sell or trade. And without that, money was in short supply. Paint peeled from walls. Iron fences began to rust and decay. Nets frayed, sails deteriorated, and the decks of boats began to buckle. If the sea suddenly began to teem with life again, the people of the Isle would have had no means to harvest it.

Billy Turner considered all of this as he sat at the docks. He surveyed the port behind him. Shuttered windows and boarded-up doors stared back.

He shook his head and ran his hands through his thick brown hair. His handsome face had grown gaunt over the past few months, and his well-toned arms were now thin and almost frail. The bright sparkle that had been evident in his blue-gray eyes when he arrived there had been extinguished, leaving in its place two despairing, brooding orbs.

A bark sounded from the far end of the

dock, and some of Billy's old joy returned for a moment.

"Crumbs!" he called out.

A ratty mutt bounded up the dock toward Billy. He was gray and white, and about the length of a retriever. Crumbs jumped up on Billy and began happily licking his face. Finally the dog sat, and Billy patted it's side. Half of Billy's joy left him again as he felt Crumbs's ribs, tight against Crumbs's skin. Crumbs was half the weight he should have been. And yet, he still seemed happy to see Billy.

"Ah, Crumbs," Billy said, smiling, "I can always count on you to pick me up."

The dog barked and jumped off Billy. Crumbs seemed to have a wealth of energy, despite his bony frame. He began to run in circles around Billy, who rose to his feet and patted the dog on his head. Using his tattered

shirtsleeve, Billy wiped the sweat from his own forehead as Crumbs began to pant.

"You want some water, then, boy? Ah, well, you've come to the right place. We've got plenty water here on the Isle of Man. Not much else, though."

He walked over to a freshwater spigot behind the dock and pumped some water out. Crumbs lapped at the spout, then nuzzled it, soaking his face. He shook the water from his head, and Billy took a drink for himself.

"Hey, ye!" a man shouted.

Whirling, Billy saw a nearly toothless man moving toward him. When he was closer, Billy noted his foul breath reeked like rotten fish.

"What makes ye think we want yer filthy dog slurpin' from the same spigot we clean our own fair skin in?"

Billy recognized the man as a member of

the *Sea Star*'s crew. The *Star* was a merchant ship having the Isle of Man as a port of call. Its crew had a particularly nasty reputation on the island. Most people kept their distance.

"He was thirsty and . . ." Billy began.

"Ah, no excuses from ye. The filthy mutt's half dead. And yet, there he goes. Drinking our clean water. Probably contaminatin' it with whatever disease it is he has there."

"It's called hunger, sir," Billy said, steeling himself for a fight. "And I hardly think that he would contaminate that there spout any more than, say, well, you and your rotten mouth."

The man's face turned a bright red, and he raised a hand toward Billy. Crumbs immediately jumped in front of his master. He growled and bared his teeth at the threatening man. Billy was impressed that the dog could still look so intimidating even in his weakened state. The man must have been equally impressed, as he dropped his fist.

"Don't ye ever let me see ye here with that dirty mutt again," the man said, pointing his finger directly at Billy's face. Billy narrowed his eyes with a steady resolve. The man was a full head taller than Billy, and twice as wide, but Billy did not back down. The man's nostrils flared before he moved to squat down and wash his face.

"Come on, Crumbs, let's go," Billy said.

As Crumbs hurried off ahead of him, Billy heard the man mumble something. He turned his attention to the man again.

"What was that?" Billy asked.

The man ignored him.

"Thought not," Billy said.

Leaving the man, he followed Crumbs up a small hill off the shore. It was only a few hundred meters to home. Billy lived with his mother's sister and her husband in a shack that was set upon a ridge. His aunt Erin, who had never cared for dogs, was a good woman, but she made Crumbs sleep outside.

She was standing at the door as Billy and Crumbs arrived. Crumbs barked and then ran around the back, where Billy had built him a doghouse.

"Oh, dear boy. You look scorched," Aunt Erin said, opening the door and welcoming Billy in. She was a slight woman, with tousled gray hair. The softness of her thick, familiar brogue comforted Billy.

She placed a hand on his shoulder and sat him down at the simple, worn table in the middle of the sparsely furnished room. The smell of the sea occasionally wafted in, mixing with the weak scent of a stew his aunt had set on the hearth.

"The heat of this must be killing you. Had I known it would've been so hot, I never would've set the hearth aflame today."

Aunt Erin made her way over to the large pot. She reached up without looking, pulled down a bowl, and ladled out a cup.

"I'm so sorry that's all I can offer you, but . . ."

Her voice broke off, and Billy could tell by her quivering mouth that she was holding back tears.

Billy looked up at her as she placed the bowl down before him.

"It's okay, really. This looks wonderful. It truly does," Billy said gently, staring at a bowl of broth that was so clear it could have been water. It was almost laughable to call it a stew. A quarter-inch slice of carrot and a sliver of celery floated around in it. Then Billy noticed that it wasn't celery at all, but a boiled maggot that must have fallen into the kettle.

Aunt Erin hovered above him.

"Well, then, go ahead and eat it," she said.

"I will. I surely will. Just waiting for it to cool down a bit," Billy said, wiping his forehead for dramatic effect before carefully pushing the bowl away.

Just then Crumbs barked loudly, and the rear door swung open. A small fish flew through the doorway into the room. It landed with a thud on the floor and flopped around, its gills laboring in the absence of the water it needed to breathe. Moments later, a short, slender man with a sheared head and a terrible sunburn entered the room.

"Was that the only one today, Uncle Seamus?" Billy asked the man, motioning to the fish, which was still flopping around.

"Only one this *week*," Uncle Seamus

replied. He unlaced his boots and set them beside the door. An unbearable stink filled the small room, and Billy tried to hide his disgust.

"So, you still can't find your skiff, then?" Uncle Seamus asked, changing the subject. He hovered over Billy and eyed his broth.

"No, sir," Billy replied. "I spent the whole of the day down at the docks searching, but it was no use."

Uncle Seamus shook his head. He leaned over Billy, then dipped into his broth and removed the maggot, popping it into his mouth.

"I tell ye, there might not be any fish here on the Isle, but ye can't complain about the hearty taste of our celery," he said.

Billy winced, but did not correct his uncle's statement. "If I can't find the skiff by week's end, I'll start to build a new one," he said instead, feeling a little queasy and eager to put an end to the conversation.

"You should've known better," Uncle Seamus said, reprimanding him. "You should've brought it back to the house. Then you'd never have to figure anything out. I'm surprised at you, Billy. There're pirates everywhere these days. They'll steal anything from you—the clothes off your back, the food you're eating; for heaven's sake, they'll even steal a worthless little skiff."

Billy was a little hurt by his uncle's calling the skiff worthless. Perhaps it was just a skiff, but it was the only boat Billy had, and probably would *ever* have. He liked to imagine that it was something grander than it really was. He had even named the little boat, painting the word *Anemone* along her side.

Uncle Seamus sat down at the table and

pulled Billy's broth close to him, digging in. The room filled with an uncomfortable silence, and Billy sensed there was something wrong.

"So ye've told 'em?" Uncle Seamus asked Aunt Erin without looking up from his bowl.

Aunt Erin grimaced and shook her head.

"Told me what?" Billy asked.

Uncle Seamus continued to eat while Aunt Erin began nervously tidying the small room.

Billy calmly folded his hands on the table and straightened his back. "I'm no longer a child. I have a right to know the matters of this household," Billy said.

Uncle Seamus pushed his empty bowl away. He looked steadily into Billy's face.

"Billy. You want to know the matters of this household? Fine, then, I'll tell you," Uncle Seamus said with a steely resolve. "We've hardly a spec of food here. I've been catchin' three or four fish a month. The house here, it's falling apart. Just last week, the floorboards on the back porch snapped, and I've not even a tenth of a pound sterling to replace them. The sea's devoid of anything but driftwood and saltwater. The town, nay, the entire *island*, is falling apart at her seams.

"Ye . . . ye've been like a son to us, William," he added. "And what I'm trying to say is . . ."

Billy closed his eyes and pinched the bridge of his nose between his thumb and forefinger.

"I know what you're trying to say," Billy said.

"I wish there were another way," Uncle Seamus said.

"There is," Billy replied, standing up from his place at the table. "You can let me help you more. We can get back on our feet. We'll move inland and start a farm. . . ."

"The farmers use seaweed for fertilizer, Billy. There's no seaweed left in the ocean. They are suffering just as greatly. No, William. The only way out of this situation is to get off the bloody island. And of the three of us, you're the best suited for that task."

Billy cringed. That was what he had feared Uncle Seamus meant. "Look at us, Billy. We're not so young. You . . . there's a lot of hope in you. So much opportunity."

Billy breathed heavily, weighed down by the gravity of the situation.

Uncle Seamus stepped up from the table and moved to the back of the shack. He kneeled down and lifted up one of the floorboards. There was a bundle of papers hidden beneath the loose board. He sorted through them and then handed one to Billy.

"What's this?" Billy asked as Uncle Seamus placed the paper in his hand.

"It's your way out. This is a ticket I purchased down on the docks. A ticket to the New World. I was well on my way to purchasing two more when the sea failed us. It will get you as far as North Carolina on the coast of America. What you do when you arrive there is your concern. All I ask is this: if you manage to make it, then send for us. The ship leaves today, lad. I wish your aunt here would have been able to bring herself to tell you sooner. To give us more time to say good-bye."

Billy looked at the piece of paper in his hand. He was overcome with so many emotions that he really didn't know how to respond. He decided to not say anything at all.

Simply nodding his head, Billy went to pack the few things he owned, and left the shack. He looked back only once, to see his aunt sobbing on her husband's shoulder and Crumbs baying mournfully on the worn-out porch. Then Billy set his eyes on the horizon and headed toward the dilapidated docks.

CHAPTER TWO

As Billy made his way to the docks, he nervously tapped the ticket against his thigh. Many merchant ships used Isle of Man as a port of call. It had once been popular for its fresh produce and ample supply of dried, salted fish. But recently, with the famine, the port had less to offer sailors, and so fewer ships were stopping there.

When Billy got down to the docks, he looked around. There were only a few ships in the harbor, and he was familiar with them all. He didn't think any of them sailed for the New World. Perhaps he'd missed his boat. A huge part of him hoped that was the case.

Near the docks, Billy saw Reverend Chambers. The reverend was a close family friend of Billy's aunt and uncle. He enjoyed fishing, boating . . . and the drink. In fact, as Billy stepped closer to him, he realized from the smell of whiskey that the reverend must have been enjoying the drink just before they'd met up.

"Billy, boy! How in blazes are ya?" Reverend Chambers asked.

"Afternoon, Reverend. I'm fine."

"Fine! Ha! So I guess then they didn't tell ya yet about shipping you off to America."

"Ah, indeed they have," Billy answered. "How is it that everyone knew about my being shipped off but me?"

The reverend shrugged and followed it up with a loud belch.

Billy hung his head, frustrated and disappointed.

"Ah, don't look so sad. And you know what, there are a few people on the Isle who didn't know. So what if they're mostly the dead ones? And by 'dead,' I mean, really dead, like lo-o-o-o-ong dead. Anyone who died in the past five years or so would've known, actually."

"This isn't making me feel much better," Billy said.

"Not here to make you feel better, lad. What do ya think I look like?"

There were a number of ways Billy could have answered that question, but he decided to remain quiet.

"Listen, Reverend, since you seem to know so much about me and my being shipped off, might you be able to tell me which ship I'm sailing on?"

In reply, Reverend Chambers sneezed in Billy's face, then wiped the snot from his nose with his sleeve. He stared blankly at Billy.

"You asking me something?" the reverend asked.

"Never mind, it's clear you're otherwise engaged."

The reverend clutched his hand to his heart as if to say he was mortally offended.

"Otherwise—otherwise . . . *what!* How could you say . . . Brian . . ."

"Billy."

"Who?"

"Me."

"What?"

"Good-bye, Reverend, I need to find my ship."

"Oh, the ship! Right! That would be the *Sea Star*."

As frustrated as he was, Billy laughed out loud. "That's very funny, Reverend."

The older man just stared at him blankly. "What's funny?" he asked.

"The joke about the *Sea Star*," Billy replied.

"Who's joking? Cheaper than a third-class ticket, that ship is. Sure, they're rough, but if you get through the voyage in one piece, you'll be in America. Beats being here, what with the sea going all empty on us, and the farms not doing much of anything, and all of those terrible drunkards. Don't you hate them drunkards?"

Billy was too distracted to say anything. He stared up at the *Sea Star*, which was still docked in the harbor. Two men were fighting in the crow's nest. One man had his hands around the other's neck, and they were struggling so violently that Billy was shocked they hadn't yet fallen out. Screams and curses and an occasional gunshot echoed from the ship. Billy felt an unpleasant tingling sensation all over his body as all the blood rushed to his head.

Was this really the boat he was expected to board? The one that would take him away from the Isle of Man? He looked back at the island. It seemed far safer and more manageable than a trip aboard this ship even despite the famine. But he didn't really have any other option. His aunt and uncle had raised him. They'd given him everything he owned and cared for him as if he were their own son. Now they were making a request, and he felt obligated to fulfill it.

Billy thanked the reverend and started to walk toward the ship.

"Hey, when you get to America, will ya

send your old reverend here some tobaccey?"

Billy waved the reverend off and continued walking toward the ship. It was as if he were in a daze. As if he were outside his body and watching the scene unfold, rather than living it. He passed stores and people, but didn't really notice any of them.

"Can I 'elp you?" a gravelly, sinister, and *familiar* voice asked from beside him.

"I'm just looking for the . . ." Billy began. His voice trailed off as he took in the owner of the voice.

"Yes?" the man answered, grinning with a mouth full of rotten teeth. It was the sailor who had threatened him and Crumbs.

The man glanced down at the ticket in Billy's hand.

"Looks like you're trying to come aboard."

Billy quickly shoved the ticket into his back pocket.

"I'm not looking for trouble. . . ."

"Oh, no, of course, *now* yer not. Now that you want to be shipmates across the wide Atlantic. Quite a long trip, mate," the man said, smiling evilly. He threw his huge arm around Billy's neck in a mock-friendly gesture. Billy was certain he'd never before felt this uncomfortable.

He slipped out from under the sailor's arm. But the man wasn't giving up easily. He planted a powerful foot in front of Billy, as if he were about to lunge toward him. Billy jumped, startled. His heart raced, and the sailor's face grew red, and he shook with laughter.

"Mr. Hawk, that will be enough," a commanding voice called from behind Billy.

Turning around, Billy saw a distinguished-looking man dressed in silk breeches and a neat tricornered hat. He carried a walking stick, and his dark curls were impeccable.

Despite his short stature, Mr. Hawk seemed to be afraid of him. He nodded, then backed away from Billy, but not before he shot him one last sneering look.

"Be on your way now, lad, and don't mix with the likes of Mr. Hawk, you hear?" the short man said, shooing Billy away with his walking stick.

"Sir, thank you, sir. Begging your pardon, though . . ." Billy stammered, still shaken by his encounter with the vicious sailor. He managed to find the ticket he'd been carrying and handed it over to the man.

The man observed Billy curiously and then took the ticket from him. He unfolded it and began to read it over. A frown crossed his face as he folded the paper and handed it back to Billy, sighing.

"Son, I'm sorry. This is worthless. Months back we caught some pirates running a scam.

They had printed up a number of these vouchers and taken advantage of the dire situation on this island. They'd hand them off to folks who would give them their entire life savings in exchange for a ticket off this vile place. Of course, in the grand scheme of things, an entire life savings here is not very much money—but still."

The man turned around to gaze at the ship, where the two men were fighting more violently than ever up in the crow's nest. "Davis! Leon!" he called out. "Cease your squabble immediately!"

If the men heard him, they did not acknowledge it.

Sighing, the man turned back to Billy and continued, "You see, even if it were a valid ticket, the *Sea Star* is not a ship you'd want to sail to America on."

Billy could hardly disagree. But his aunt

and uncle had spent every last dime they had to get Billy off the island in the hopes that at some point he could send for them. And that, he felt, was something worth fighting for. He owed them at least that much.

The man turned toward the ship again.

"Davis! Leon! If you do not kill each other, I will see to it that you are put to death before we leave port this evening!"

Hearing the man's words, it occurred to Billy that he must be someone in a high position aboard the ship.

"Sir, certainly there must be something you can do to get me aboard. It's of the utmost urgency that I get to America," he pleaded.

"I may be the *Sea Star*'s captain, but I can't just let anyone aboard that wants to come aboard."

Had Billy heard correctly?

"Captain?" Billy said, with a little more

awe than he would have liked.

"Yes—captain—but I have an agency to answer to. I'm sorry, lad. I can't honor this ticket, and I can't take you aboard."

Just then, an incredibly loud creaking and cracking sound, like that of a ship running itself clear into a reef, sounded from beside the dock. It was followed by a couple of inhuman screeches. Billy whipped around to see that the *Sea Star*'s crow's nest had split apart. The two men who had been fighting in it had come tumbling out and were falling.

The captain's eyes widened.

Billy felt as if he were going to be sick.

There was a disgusting *splat* as the two men hit the deck. The captain winced, and Billy covered his eyes. There followed an ungodly quiet, which lasted a few seconds, before the ship returned to its regular buzz of cursing, banter, and gun blasts.

The captain turned to Billy.

"Can you hoist sails?"

"I've no idea."

"Do you know how to rig a ship?"

"I'm a quick learner."

"Name?"

"Billy. Billy Turner."

"I'm short two men, Billy Turner," the captain said. "Do you think you can pull the weight of two good—if somewhat hostile and often drunk—men?"

"I can surely try," Billy said, his face beginning to brighten, though it was still mixed with a little bit of fear.

"Well then, I'm Captain David Donovan. Welcome to the crew of the *Sea Star*, Billy Turner."

CHAPTER THREE

On his first morning on the *Sea Star*, Billy awakened at the sound of a loud bell. He was disoriented for a moment, not quite sure where he was. Shifting he pulled the dirty, rough, wool blanket he'd been given over his head.

Just as Billy began to fall back to sleep, the bell rang out again. This time, it was followed by the loud barking of an officer of the ship.

"All hands on deck!" the officer shouted.

Billy opened his eyes again and adjusted to his surroundings. Everything came flooding back to him: the docks, the ticket to America, the captain, and the *Sea Star*. He had hoped it was all a terrible dream.

Billy was used to waking before dawn. Back on the Isle of Man, the bait had needed to be sorted and the nets prepared long before the day got started. But somehow, waking early on the *Sea Star* was different. As the newest member of the crew, Billy was made to sleep belowdecks on the floor in a far corner of the ship. He did not have a cabin of his own, or even a bunk.

Billy dusted himself off and followed some of the other sailors that were sharing his less than desirable quarters. They filed up a rickety staircase, and upon emerging from below, Billy had to squint to block the early-morning light.

Once on deck, the crew seemed to mill about. Some men were already swilling grog. Captain Donovan stood on top of a crate and barked orders at the crew. "You've each got a job to do, and you each know what that job is," he shouted over the din of the sailors, some of whom were chatting, others laughing—some of whom were even snoring on their feet. "Get to those jobs now, men, or you'll be appropriately punished," he said.

"Punishment? You mean we'll need to eat whatever stomach-turning meal Hawk's turning out tonight," someone in the crowd heckled.

The captain's face grew serious, and despite his short stature and polished clothing, Billy found himself feeling—not for the first time—a bit frightened of him.

"No, Jameson," the captain said. "In fact, those punished won't be eating much of

35

anything at all, save whatever fish you might find in Davy Jones's Locker. This ship is fitted with a plank, and I have no reservations about using it. And remember, we are approximately two hundred leagues from any significant landmass."

The crew quieted down and between growls and grunts began to shuffle off to their various duties. The captain looked severe, but satisfied. Billy was still reeling from the strictness the captain had shown the crew when Donovan approached him.

"Mr. Turner," the captain said.

"Captain," Billy replied.

"You should be particularly cautious, son. We have no problem starting with the newest crew members first when finding candidates to walk the plank," Captain Donovan said.

"But . . ." Billy objected, confused.

"*But?* You dare 'but' a captain," he said, his face turning beet red. "Men, ready the plank!"

"Sir, with all due respect, you don't understand," Billy began. "I have no trouble working. You told me I'd need to pull the weight of two sailors, and I agreed. But—"

"Then what is the problem?" the captain said, cutting him off.

"If you'll let me finish, sir," Billy said, as politely as he could.

The captain seemed to take this as an affront, and gave Billy a warning glance.

"You've not told me what my role, or roles, as the case may be, aboard this ship *is*," Billy finished, heaving a sigh of relief at having finally said his piece.

"Boy, you'll need to learn to speak up!" the captain shouted at him. "This is exactly the type of lackluster behavior I am speaking about. It was your duty to tell me that at the beginning of this journey."

"I *tried*," Billy pleaded.

"Never mind it now. I will let this one instance go," the captain said. Then he began to walk away.

"Sir!" Billy called out to him.

"Yes, Mr. Turner," the captain said, turning around, his jaw clenched.

"If I may ask, then, what *is* my role?"

"You should know, Turner," the captain said.

"But you haven't *told* me yet."

"That's no excuse," the captain said.

Billy was confused, not to mention very frustrated. His eyes widened, and he turned his head to one side, as if to say, *I have no idea where else to go with this conversation.*

"You are in the kitchen. Executive assistant to our cook, Mr. Hawk," the captain said.

Billy's eyes widened even more. He

opened his mouth to object but was quickly interrupted by the captain.

"Something to say then, lad?"

Billy thought better of it, given the captain's earlier rant about walking the plank.

"Good, then. I'll look forward to dinner this evening," the captain said. He tipped his hat to Billy and walked away, twirling his walking stick a little as he went.

Billy sighed. He thought about how much his life had changed in such a short time. Not even twenty-four hours before, he'd been petting Crumbs on the docks of the Isle of Man, and now . . . well, now he was stuck at sea with a boatload of cutthroats and a captain who was clearly insane.

Billy looked around. There really was no land as far as the eye could see. He needed to make the best of his situation. There was no other option.

Billy wasn't exactly sure where the kitchen was. He asked a few men on deck, but received only grunts of irritation in response. Eventually, he returned belowdecks and followed the sound of crashing pots and pans. At the end of a long, dark corridor, he found the galley. Inside, he could make out Mr. Hawk bounding around. Billy walked up to within about ten feet of the doorway and hesitated.

"I know yer there. Show yerself!" Mr. Hawk said, without turning around.

Billy slowly made his way into the kitchen.

"You!" Mr. Hawk said.

Billy shrugged.

"What is it ye want, then?" Mr. Hawk asked.

"On captain's orders, I'm here to assist you in the galley," Billy replied.

Mr. Hawk let out a sidesplitting laugh.

Then his smile vanished and was replaced by a fixed stare.

"Yer not kidding, are ye?" he asked.

"No, sir," Billy replied.

"Ye know," Mr. Hawk said, "I should kill ye."

Billy steeled himself.

"In fact, I should skin yer alive fer the way ye talked to me back on the Isle," the cook continued.

Billy returned Mr. Hawk's gaze and tried to appear calm. He could not deny that he was frightened, but he was also not going to apologize for mouthing off to Mr. Hawk when the cook had deserved every word of it.

"I have to say that it was pretty dumb of ye to come at a man of me size like that, the way ye did, y'know. But it was also pretty brave," Mr. Hawk said finally.

Billy wasn't sure of what to say. He decided

"Thank you" was the most appropriate choice.

Hawk nodded at the salutation. "Now, don't get to thinking this means we're friends, because we're nothing of the sort, lad. I'm just saying, if we're gonna need to be workin 'ere together, we might as well start fresh, ye know?"

Mr. Hawk picked up a heavy sack of potatoes and casually tossed it at Billy. The force of the sack overwhelmed him, and he fell to the floor, potatoes spilling every which way.

"Pick 'em up. All of 'em, and start peeling," Mr. Hawk commanded. "And then start on these 'ere dishes."

Much to Billy's surprise, the weeks seemed to fly by quickly—and rather smoothly. This was helped in no small part by the fact that despite what Mr. Hawk had said about not being Billy's friend, he had wound up being Billy's chief defender. No one on the crew dared antagonize Billy while Mr. Hawk was around.

Mr. Hawk seemed to have taken a genuine liking to Billy, who was reliable and hard-working. He'd told Billy on a number of occasions that the galley had never been in better order. The quality of the food aboard the ship had markedly improved. And Mr. Hawk seemed generally to be in a better mood than he had been when Billy first met him.

Over the weeks, he'd taught Billy sailor chanteys and had told him that it was said that some of them had secret meanings, embedded by pirates and apparently recorded in a mysterious book called the *Pirata Codex*. Mr. Hawk thought that the hidden messages and such were just old wives' tales. But he warned Billy that it was probably better not to take a chance singing the songs in public.

If there *were* secret messages encoded in them, he might be mistaken for a pirate and attacked or, worse, killed.

Because of all this, Billy was a bit sad in part that the journey would soon come to an end. Any day now they were due to land in Bermuda. And from there, it was only a short trip to North Carolina. Not only had he formed a very strong bond with Mr. Hawk, but he also fancied he'd made quite an impression on the captain. He found it difficult to believe, but he actually thought he might miss this crew. At least a little bit.

The morning that they were scheduled to dock in Bermuda, Billy got up extra early. He positioned himself at the bow of the ship and looked out to sea. Dawn was just beginning to break, and everything seemed peaceful. He appeared to be the only member of the crew up and about, and the quietness of the deck combined with the stillness of the sea filled him with an ease he had not experienced since before he left the Isle of Man.

He took a very deep breath, wanting to feel the clean salt air inside him. But he quickly gagged and began to cough. The air was not clean and salty at all. It smelled like rotten fish that had been left to fester, heaped in the sun for weeks. Billy leaned over the edge of the ship and heaved.

With blurry eyes, he looked out to sea, and what he saw there took him aback. Hundreds, maybe thousands, of fish of all kinds, all sizes, floating on the surface. Some were mutilated; others looked as if they'd simply died. Seagulls hovered high above the area, squawking, but none dared to descend and take part in the fetid meal.

Then Billy saw something move. He

wasn't sure exactly what it was, but it was clearly a sea creature, and it was clearly alive. Its huge arcing back dipped under the waves and out of sight. Could it have been a whale? Or a particularly large eel? He wasn't sure. But whatever it was, it seemed to have escaped the fate of its smaller brethren.

As quickly as it had come into view, the terrible scene was out of sight. And just as Billy was getting ready to inform the captain about it, the bell near the crow's nest began to ring.

"Land ho!" a sailor cried out.

"Aye!" the sailors on the deck hollered back.

And there, just ahead of the *Sea Star*, Billy saw Bermuda appearing on the horizon, as if it were rising from the ocean herself.

CHAPTER FOUR

Before long, the thin line of the horizon had become bigger, bolder, and greener. The sailors aboard the *Sea Star* were furiously readying the ship to dock in the port, which was now visible at the southern end of the small peninsula they were sailing around. A British flag flapped in the wind high above the docks. The same flag waved from the mast of the *Sea Star*, though the ship's flag was far more weatherworn than the pristine one raised over Bermuda.

As they sailed closer, it seemed to Billy as if the port itself were moving toward the ship, and not the other way around. Approaching land, small red shapes began to grow larger until Billy began to recognize them as men. Then, as they moved in even closer, Billy realized that they were members of the Royal Navy.

Deep inside him, something relaxed. While he had grown accustomed to life aboard the ship, and even become friendly with Mr. Hawk and the captain, he was still uneasy with the rough crew. For the first time since they'd departed the Isle of Man, Billy felt completely safe. If anything *did* go wrong, the soldiers would be there to help him.

Mr. Hawk stepped up beside Billy and laid one of his large hands on his shoulder.

"Ah, much as I love the sea, there's nothing

like the feeling of firm ground beneath your feet," he said, smiling.

Billy turned and nodded in agreement.

Mr. Hawk leaned over the railing and took a deep breath.

"And smell that air," he said. "Not just fresh salt air, but air mixed with sand and soil, and grass. Haven't smelled those things in a while, eh, mate?"

Billy smiled. "Has been quite some time," he said. "How long will we be docked here?"

Mr. Hawk didn't reply. His attention was focused on the pier—and the redcoats. And his expression was now filled with concern. Billy thought it might even be worry.

"Mr. Hawk, what's wrong?" Billy asked.

"Nothing, lad. Nothing at all," Mr. Hawk said.

Before Billy could press him any further, Captain Donovan appeared behind them.

"Men. Mr. Hawk, in particular," he said. "Can you please tell me what's going on here?"

Mr. Hawk shook his head rapidly.

"I—I don't know, sir."

"Well somebody had better. How are we to continue under these circumstances?" the captain asked.

"We do have the papers from Ipswich," Mr. Hawk replied.

"Do you honestly believe those to be usable?"

"They've worked before," Mr. Hawk said.

Billy didn't quite know what was going on, but he was growing uneasy with the shady banter. And as he looked toward the dock to the navy officers and soldiers below, to reassure himself, he became even more concerned. The men had severe, harsh looks on their faces.

As the *Sea Star* pulled into dock, one of the higher-ranking officers stepped forward.

"Permission to dock, sir," Captain Donovan said.

The officer stared back in stony silence.

"Where is Admiral Lawson?" the captain forged on.

The officer broke his silence.

"Admiral Lawson has been hanged. He was found to have been allowing use of this port by pirates in exchange for compensation from said pirate fiends. In the eyes of the crown, this makes him a pirate himself. But then, perhaps you know all that already. Perhaps he was helping your own pirate ship run goods as well."

The captain stood firm.

"Sir, I assure you we are not a pirate ship. I run a vessel of good men here," he said.

Behind him a fight had broken out, and a sailor was swearing loudly, while holding his broken nose.

The captain cleared his throat and turned his attention back to the docks.

"We request dockage."

"Whether you were free to dock was never a question," the officer said ominously. "What will happen to you after you do dock is the true matter at hand."

After disembarking, the crew of the *Sea Star* lined up on the dock. For every sailor, there was a soldier standing before him with a gun pointed at his face. Billy stared down the barrel before him. His knees shook and his eyes crossed, the gun being so close to his face.

He had been separated from the captain and Mr. Hawk, who were now at the opposite end of the line. Close beside them was the admiral who had apparently replaced Lawson. Billy tried to lean over to see if the officer was questioning the captain, but he accidently butted his eye against the gun barrel before him and started back.

"Captain," he heard the officer begin, "you and your men are docking in a port known to be frequented by pirates, searching for an officer who was recently executed for piracy. Prove your innocence or suffer his fate."

The captain spoke up, "Men, produce your papers!"

Billy heard shuffling and shifting and crumbling all around him. What papers were they looking for? His chest tightened. He was certain that he didn't have the papers that were being requested. He reached into his pocket and pulled out the only paper he had—the counterfeit ticket that Uncle Seamus had given him.

As each sailor produced his papers, the gun before him was dropped.

"See, officer? We're a law-abiding ship," the captain said.

"Papers!" a soldier shouted into Billy's face.

Billy's ticket quivered in his hand as he raised it up to the soldier, who tore it from his hand, examined it, and then called the admiral over. The two mumbled something, and then the soldier grabbed Billy by the arm and threw him to the ground. Billy landed facedown in the dirt as the admiral stormed over.

"Pirate!" the admiral said accusingly.

"No, sir, there's a mistake, I'm not a . . ."

"Silence!" the admiral shouted.

Billy tried to stand up, but the big, booted foot of a soldier came crashing down upon his head, forcing his face back into the dirt.

The admiral stormed back over to the captain, waving the counterfeit ticket in his face.

"So, not pirates, then?" the admiral barked. "As you most likely know already, this is a fraudulent document, printed by pirates. What say you?"

"Which man of mine produced this vile thing?" the captain asked angrily.

"The skinny one, down at the other end," Mr. Hawk replied, before any of the navy men could.

Billy's heart raced. What was Mr. Hawk doing?

"Boy!" Captain Donovan shouted. He stormed over to Billy. "Who are you? What are you doing aboard my ship?"

Billy's mood went quickly from shocked and confused to furious.

"Come now, Captain, you know exactly who I am. You're the one who took me aboard . . ." Billy replied.

"Quite the contrary! I have never before

seen you in my life. A stowaway you are. And a pirate! The likes of you make my blood boil."

Billy turned to the admiral to plead his case.

"He's lying! I showed him this ticket and he told me it was counterfeit. He was going to refuse me passage, but two of his men killed each other and he needed me aboard. Hawk, tell him!" Billy shouted, his face growing redder.

But Hawk just stared at Billy with a quizzical expression. "How do you know my name?" he asked Billy.

"Must have been skulking around our cabins without our knowing. Listening in on our conversations," the captain said disgustedly.

"What are you on about?" Billy shouted.

The captain didn't answer. "Take this man away and do what you will with him!

Men of his ilk—these *pirates*—turn my stomach!" he said to the admiral's men.

The soldiers grabbed Billy by the arms and lifted him up. One bound his hands and feet in chains, while a half dozen others aimed their guns at him.

"Are we free to go, then?" the captain said.

The admiral considered the question.

"Are you certain you have no other *stowaways* aboard?" he asked.

"As certain as one can be," Captain Donovan answered, flashing a brilliant smile.

"Then, yes, you are free to go about your business," the admiral said.

"What will become of the pirate?" Mr. Hawk asked.

"He'll be taken to Port Royal, where he'll be hanged and displayed as an example of what fate lies in store for his kind."

Billy glared at Hawk. If there was any

regret about Billy's demise in the cook's face, Billy couldn't see it.

The captain held Billy by the chin and spat into his face. As the spittle dripped down his cheek, Billy's anger grew so severe that he thought he'd break through his bonds and kill the man. But his hands were bound in iron, and no anger, no matter how strong, could have broken those chains.

The admiral, who had not taken his eyes off Billy the whole time, leaned in once more.

"Welcome to Bermuda, pirate," he said. "Enjoy it while you can. In a week's time you'll not be able to enjoy anything at all. In a week's time—you'll be dead."

CHAPTER FIVE

*A*ll too quickly, Billy found himself in a fortified cell surrounded by soldiers. The cell had a dirt floor and was very small, perhaps six feet long by three feet wide. At one end of the tiny space was a gate with a loophole that had been fastened with an iron lock. At the other end was a small, barred window. The remaining walls were constructed of solid brick.

The window allowed things from the

outside world into his cell: pale moonlight, the smell of the sea, and, most unfortunately, the jovial sound of the sailors from the *Sea Star* having a good time on the town. Above the other voices he could hear Mr. Hawk's drunken cackling.

Leaning against the wall under the window, Billy sank down to the dusty floor. He tugged at his hair and hit his fist against his thigh in frustration. How could he have been so trusting? He had come to think of them not only as crewmembers, but also as friends. But now they were free, and he was locked up. He couldn't remember a time when he had ever felt so betrayed.

Billy's eyes grew heavy as sleep threatened to overtake him. But every time his eyes closed, a heavy, sweaty guard would rap on the gate with his rifle, making sure Billy didn't enjoy anything, including a moment's rest.

"Tired, eh, mate?" the guard asked.

Billy glared at him.

"Well, ye should've thought of that before ye became a pirate!"

"I'm. No. Pirate," Billy stated through clenched teeth.

The guard took a bite from a large, juicy peach. The nectar dripped down his cheek and all over the front of his uniform.

"Admiral says ye are one," the man said, bits of peach flying from his mouth as he spoke.

"Well, the *admiral*'s wrong," Billy snapped.

"Hold yer tongue, boy," the guard said, moving in close and spraying Billy with spit and bits of peach.

Before Billy could respond, he heard a group of men marching down the corridor toward his cell. He pressed his face against the bars and strained to see them. It was the admiral and a group of soldiers.

"Billiam Turner!" the admiral called out.

"Billy," Billy said, correcting him.

"What?"

"My name is Billy. Or William. It's not Billiam," Billy said.

"Are you mocking me?" the admiral barked.

"No, I'm merely correcting you," Billy said innocently.

The admiral set his jaw, then smiled grimly.

"You'll hang in a few days. And then your name—like your pathetic little life—will be of no matter. Guards, bring him out to the brig."

The huge guard wiped his hands on his trousers, then reached for his iron keys. He unlocked the door and whipped it open. Two other men reached into the cell and grabbed Billy—one by the arm, the other by the hair—and dragged him out of the cell. As they marched him past the other holding cells, drunken men who looked far more like pirates than Billy did spat and cursed at him.

It was only a short walk from the prison to the ship that would take Billy to Port Royal. Ten men walked ahead of Billy, and a group of at least that many trailed behind him. As they marched to the ship under the clear night sky, townsfolk booed and hissed at him. Then he spotted the crew of the *Sea Star*. Billy locked eyes with Mr. Hawk. The cook didn't gloat, nor did he seem happy that Billy had been taken prisoner. But he was clearly not saddened by his situation, either.

A soldier kicked Billy in the rear to move him along. Billy gave Mr. Hawk one last look and shook his head. All too soon he was making his way up the mahogany gangplank of an elegant navy ship. Once he was in the ship, however, he realized that there were parts of it that were definitely not elegant at all. Especially the brig.

Not fifteen minutes earlier, Billy had been thinking that he would rather be anywhere but in his cell. But as he neared the brig, he was suddenly wishing he were back there. The brig stank. The floor was covered in sludge. The ceiling dripped with a yellowish brown liquid. One of the guards opened the gate and held a torch up to illuminate the cell. It was filled with rats, gnawing at the walls. Catching Billy's disgusted stare, the admiral smiled.

With no fanfare, Billy was thrown face-down into the sludge. He thought that the rats would scurry away upon his arrival. But his new cell-mates proved very stubborn. They simply bared their fangs and appeared to hiss at him. They weren't going any-where. As if to prove the point, he felt a sharp pain in his foot and kicked back. A rat had bitten right through the leather of his boot! He kicked harder, and the rodent flew right off his foot and through the air, landing squarely on the admiral's face.

Screaming, the admiral grabbed the rat in one hand and threw it right back into Billy's cell. Then he seized Billy by the shoulder, raised the butt of his gun, and brought it down on Billy's head. The world went black.

The next thing Billy heard was murmuring. He realized that he must have been knocked out, but had no idea for how long. His head was throbbing; he attempted to rub the tenderest part, but quickly realized his hands had not been untied as they had been when he had been thrown into the other cell.

With a great effort, Billy managed to open an eye to take a look around.

His cell in the brig had been closed and locked. The guards seemed to be gone. Beyond his cell, torchlight flickered on the filthy walls. Now he could make out something else—shadows of hunched figures. They seemed to be moving closer. The mumbling seemed to be coming closer as well.

Could it be more guards?

No, the shadows looked far too small to be guards. And the voices sounded young. One even sounded like . . . a girl's?

"Ye know, I really don't feel quite right about this," the voice said. It definitely belonged to a girl.

Billy closed his eyes and pretended to be knocked out. He wasn't sure what was going on, but he certainly did not want to get mixed up with girls who were not feeling right about things aboard navy ships. What was a girl even *doing* on a navy ship in the first place? Billy had landed himself in enough trouble since leaving the Isle of Man. This newest development could only get him in deeper. Women on ships were bad luck.

"You don't feel right, *mon chere*?" a boy's voice said. "You know, you're really going to have to change that outlook. We've joined the crew of a pirate ship. We're going to have to do some things that might not seem so right."

Pirates! Billy's eyes flew open. He'd be hanged on the spot if the navy caught pirates lurking around his cell.

Apparently unaware of, or unconcerned by, his presence, the boy and the girl continued their conversation.

"I understand that now and then we might have to bend the rules a bit. But stealing from the navy? Don't ye think that's a wee bit extreme?" the girl asked.

"Oh, come now. As Jack would say, we're not really stealing . . ." the boy replied.

"Oh, don't ye bring Jack Sparrow into this. That boy is a few sails short of a ship, if ye know what I mean."

Billy didn't like where this conversation was going.

"Besides," the girl continued, "we have sneaked on to a vessel belonging to the Crown, we are planning to break into a cabin on that very vessel, and once we break into that cabin we are going to find something that doesn't belong to us and take it. Now, ye tell me, how is that *not* stealing?"

Billy was convinced. And so, it seemed, was the girl's partner.

"Okay," the boy said, sighing, "it's stealing. But if we don't do it, your *maman* will be quite, er, how would you say . . . mad! And we all know what she's like when she's angry."

Billy could practically hear the girl shiver. What was going on? Two pirates, no older than teenagers, with some sort of moral code and a mother who would be angry if they *didn't* steal something? Billy had never heard anything like this before.

"Let's try over here," the boy said.

The figures came even closer to Billy's cell. He had to do something. He couldn't risk being caught with pirates. It would wipe away any slim chance he had of surviving this situation.

A foot tiptoed in front of his cell. Billy jammed his elbow down on the tail of one of the rats that was nearest to him. The rat screeched. The girl screamed. Billy lifted up his head and took a first look at the pair.

In the dim light he could tell the girl was pretty but a bit worn, with long, wavy, auburn hair. The boy was a full head shorter than she was. His reddish brown hair was curly, and his full face was freckled.

"Hello," Billy said.

"Ye fiend! Who are ye?" the girl asked.

"I don't think I'm the fiend here. You are, after all, the ones looking for something to steal," he pointed out.

"Arabella," the boy said, grabbing the girl's arm, "the crew must have heard you scream. We need to get out of here. Quick!"

Billy held the girl's gaze. He was done for. The navy would find these pirates and think they were trying to help him escape. Then they'd do away with all three of them at once. There was only one action to take.

"Please, take me with you," Billy begged. "Help me escape."

The girl appeared to be taken aback.

"And why should we do that? Ye criminal!"

"Again, *I'm* not the one looking to rob the navy."

"What was yer crime, then?" Arabella asked.

"I'm accused of being a pirate. But I'm not!" Billy said. Then he remembered who it was that he was speaking to. "Not that there's anything wrong with being a pirate. Look, they are planning to hang me in Port Royal. But I've done nothing wrong."

"That does sound like the navy," the boy said.

"Why should we believe ye?" Arabella asked.

"If you don't, and I am telling the truth, then an innocent man will hang in Port Royal. And *you'll* have let it happen," Billy answered.

"That's very unfair to position it that way," Arabella said.

"Arabella, if we do release him, and he is

telling the truth, we'll have an ally when it comes time to fight our way through the navy crew."

Arabella gave Billy a curious look. For a moment, it seemed she might acquiesce. But then she shook her head.

"No, let's go, Jean," Arabella said. "We need to find the room where the criminal records are kept. And so far, all we've found is the ship's sewage outlet."

"Is that what smells so bad down here?" Jean asked.

"If it weren't mum's first mate who had been taken prisoner by the navy, you know I'd not even be down here. I'm not freeing criminals on top of it all," Arabella said.

"I know where the records are kept," Billy lied, thinking quickly.

That seemed to interest Arabella. Jean looked equally interested. Raising an eyebrow,

Arabella nodded to Jean, who took a ring of keys out of his pocket. The head of each was sculpted to look like a different skull.

"I knew I wasn't wasting my doubloons when I picked up these skeleton keys in New Orleans," he said.

Jean unlocked the cell and freed Billy of his bonds, helping him to his feet. He wiped his hands on his pants to get the sludge off.

"I'm Billy . . . Billy Turner."

"I'm Arabella Smith," the girl said, "and this is Jean Magliore. We sail under Captain Laura Smith, aboard the *Fleur de la Mort*. And fer the record, I still don't trust ye."

"I haven't yet given you reason to," Billy said.

"Let's fix that," Arabella said.

Billy nodded. A good way to start would be to find the records room. He just wished he knew where it was.

CHAPTER SIX

*B*illy's initial fears that the navy would come looking for him after hearing Arabella's scream were not borne out. In fact, most of the guards appeared to have been sleeping, and a few were even drunk. For this reason, sneaking past them by the stairwell leading out of the brig and up onto the deck was not difficult. The two guards stationed there seemed to be both drunk *and* sleeping.

"Er, the records room should be down this

way, if I remember correctly," Billy said, leading Arabella and Jean down the path that lay immediately before him.

"Let's go, then," Arabella said. But after a few brisk steps, she halted.

"What's the matter?" Billy asked.

"Who's to say that ye aren't going to lead us to the admiral or some other navy person?"

Billy laughed, trying not to sound nervous. "Why would I do that?" he asked. "After all, the navy is after me, too."

"Yeah, sure. But ye turn us in, and ye've given the navy two pirates. You Parlay with them, ask them to grant you amnesty in return fer us, and ye're free to go."

Billy stared at Arabella blankly. The thought of turning the pair in hadn't even crossed his mind.

"Great, *chérie*," Jean said to Arabella, reading Billy's expression. "If our new friend did not intend to turn us in before, he might be tempted to now."

"Look, I've no desire to turn either one of you in. I'd simply like to help you find the papers you seek and get off this ship before I can be hanged," Billy said in a soft, slow voice.

"Why even help us find our papers? Yer already free. Why don't you just jump ship now?" Arabella asked skeptically.

"Arabella, you're not really making this any easier. Can't we just accept that maybe he's willing to help?" Jean whispered.

"Besides," Billy said, nodding, "I do owe you the favor. You freed me from the brig."

"Ah, so now yer masquerading around as a man with honor. There's nothing worse than that—a man with none acting like he's got all of it in the world."

Arabella stormed ahead. Jean hung back.

"She has issues with trust, *mon ami*," Jean

whispered. Then, in an even lower voice, he said, "I believe you're going to help, though. So lead us to our documents!"

Billy smiled weakly.

"*This* door?" Arabella hissed a moment later, doing her best to keep her voice down.

Billy hesitated, then nodded. This was the moment of truth.

Jean's eyes lit up, and he darted toward Arabella. Billy increased his pace and joined them at the door. Jean once again took his skeleton keys, and tried a few of them. The first four didn't work, but with a turn of the fifth, the lock clicked open. Jean smiled slyly. Billy hoped that of all the cabins on the ship, he'd chosen the right one.

Jean gripped the door handle and opened the door slowly. The three leaned in—and an awful stench filled their noses. The room was dark. Arabella looked at Billy and raised an eyebrow. Billy took a breath, unintentionally inhaling the awful smell of the cabin. He began to cough.

"Well, whatever it is in there, it certainly doesn't smell like documents," Jean observed.

Billy surveyed the room. As he stepped in, a loud *squawk* burst out from somewhere inside. It was quickly followed by others. The sound of wings flapping filled the tiny cabin, and feathers began to swirl around Billy.

"I think you've found the chicken coop!" Jean said.

Billy rushed to shut the door before the sound of the birds woke anyone on the ship.

"Trying to cause a ruckus so that we're discovered?" Arabella said.

"Look, I thought they were in here. They took me into the document room when we boarded, to log in my capture," Billy lied. "I was tired, hungry, beaten up a little bit . . . It was a room that looked like this. That's all I know."

"I say we send ye back to the brig," Arabella said. "Yer no help to us. Ye might even be a liability."

Billy looked desperately to Jean.

"Why don't we give him another chance? I can see how someone in his state could mistake this room for another."

Arabella shrugged, but agreed to give Billy another chance. And another and another and another. But after opening the door to a room filled with dirty underwear, then another that reeked of rotten cabbage, another that was completely empty, and another that was completely full (causing the contents to spill out of the door when it was opened), Arabella had had enough.

"We could be doing this all ourselves, ye know? Stumbling around the ship like dolts going from door to door guessing where the documents are. Look, I'm giving ye one more chance. Then I'm afraid we have no choice but to ask ye to leave, whether it be by returning to the brig or walking the plank."

Arabella seemed quite sincere about this, and Jean shrugged at Billy, clearly unable to reassure him.

"Okay, look, now I'm remembering more clearly. It's that room. The one right down this corridor, with the small window. The one with the torches on either side of the door."

"Are ye absolutely *sure*?" Arabella asked sternly.

"I'm sure," Billy said, dropping his eyes to the deck. He realized that if he were wrong, he'd be killed—either by these two young pirates or by the navy. He didn't know which would be worse.

Arabella nodded. Jean made his way down

the corridor, with Arabella and Billy close behind. As before, when they got to the door, Jean looked and fidgeted with his skeleton keys. He slipped in a key that looked about right for the hole. He turned it, and the lock clicked. But his expression showed confusion rather than satisfaction.

"What's the matter, Jean?" Arabella whispered.

"*La porte*—the door—it clicked," Jean answered.

"I know it did, we're standing right here," Arabella said.

"Now, I mean, it clicked *locked*," Jean said.

Arabella hurried over and took the keys from Jean's hand. She searched for the one he'd used and held it up to the torches.

"Is *this* the key ye locked the door with?" Arabella asked.

"*Oui,*" Jean answered as Arabella tried to

quickly stick it in the keyhole. "But what are you doing?"

"I just want to get what we're here for and get off this ship. So far we've accumulated a fugitive and broken into five navy rooms—six if ye include the brig!"

"But the fact that it was open," Billy began, reaching out to stop her. "It means there is probably—"

Before he could finish, Arabella flung the door open. It was the records room, all right, filled to the ceiling with papers, books, and ledgers. And there was something else in there, too. Something they did not expect to find.

The admiral!

"Oh, my stars . . ." Arabella said, stunned, as the admiral drew his sword and ran at the three of them.

"Pirates!" he yelled. "Come to save one of

your own? Now you will *all* perish by the Sword of Justice!"

The three did not need any further encouragement. They took off.

As the admiral ran after them, he violently jerked the clapper of every bell he passed on deck, signaling his men to wake up and come to arms. And in case that wasn't loud enough, he also yelled—a lot.

Navy sailors darted from their rooms, most of them in disordered uniforms, some half dressed, but all of them armed.

"I don't know who I am more terrified of," Jean said to Arabella, "the navy or your mother. Once she finds out we don't have the records in hand *and* we've upset the navy, she'll have us walk the *Fleur de la Mort*'s plank."

"Mum . . ." Arabella repeated fearfully. She ran to the broadside of the ship and called out into the empty night, "Mum! Come aboard! And bring all the arms you can carry!"

Billy couldn't believe it. Just when he thought that his experiences since leaving the Isle of Man couldn't get any stranger, he found himself aboard a navy ship watching a girl, a *pirate* girl, no less, call out into the emptiness for her mother. There were no ships, no lights, no anything, for as far as the eye could see. There weren't even the sounds you might expect to hear if another ship were nearby. No bells, no crew scurrying around, no sails flapping. They were alone on this ocean. So who did this insane girl think she was talking to?

What Billy saw next caused him to believe that perhaps it wasn't the girl who was crazy, but rather, himself.

As he stared at the dark night that

surrounded Arabella, two pirates—a boy who looked Mayan and a tall, imposing woman—dived out of thin air and landed on the deck with two heroic thuds. Those sounds were followed close behind by another thud. This one was much quieter; Billy realized that something small and furry had followed them from wherever they came from. Could it be a cat? It looked more like a huge, miserable rat.

The woman who had emerged from thin air looked very much like Arabella. Billy guessed that she was in fact Arabella's mother, and a tough cookie at that. She held a sword in each hand and wore two more on her hips. The boy—who was about Jean's height and age—was wielding what appeared to be an obsidian knife.

The woman tossed the swords in her hands to Arabella and Jean, who caught them with ease.

The thing—which did in fact seem to be a cat—ran up to Billy and hissed.

"No, Constance!" Jean called to the cat. "He's on our side!"

"So says ye!" Arabella shouted just as the pursuing navy men came upon them. The sound of steel against steel filled the night as swords clanked all around.

An all-out battle had broken out between the *Fleur*'s small group of pirates and the navy, and the pirates were doing an amazingly good job of holding their own. They were outnumbered at least twenty to one, but they seemed to fight much more effectively than the navy, using unusual tactics to overcome their opponents.

Jean lowered a series of ballasts that were hanging in the rigging onto a group of sailors, taking five of them out at once. The boy with the obsidian knife severed one of the ratlines, netting a good twenty men in one fell swoop. He quickly tied the line into knots, trapping the sailors inside. Even the cat, Constance, seemed to be making the most of her opportunities. She weaved in and out among the sailors' legs, tripping them up and allowing Jean, Arabella, and the others to profit by her work.

Billy was not sure exactly what he should do. If he fought with the pirates and they lost, he would be done for by the navy. If he fought with the navy, he'd be done for by the pirates. If he took no action at all, he'd most likely be executed in Port Royal.

He thought about it for a moment, and then caught a glimpse of the admiral, battling with Arabella's mother, Laura Smith. Both of them looked severe and violent. But there was a nastiness, maybe even an evilness, in the admiral's eyes. He seemed to want to beat the pirates for the sake of killing them and getting the credit. Laura, on the other hand, looked as if she were battling for her life. She looked as though she really believed in something. Billy had no idea what that something was, but he was beginning to believe that perhaps pirate and honest sailor, like good and bad, were not as easy to distinguish as he'd been taught.

At that moment he decided to do something he would never have considered doing even a month prior. Billy Turner, a fisherman from the Isle of Man, decided to become a pirate.

And just as he made that momentous decision, Billy realized that the battle had taken everyone to the front end of the ship. The records room was on the aft end. Every sailor on the ship was engaged in the battle with the pirates, which meant that the records room was left unguarded.

He sneaked down the corridor they had so recently traversed and located the room. The door was still unlocked. It swayed open and closed as the boat rocked back and forth on the waves with the motion of the battle.

He grabbed a torch from alongside the room and entered. There were papers everywhere, and Billy held the torch as close as possible, knowing that if he weren't careful he would set the whole room aflame. He didn't know where to begin, but soon realized that the papers were filed by ship name. Arabella had said her mother's vessel was called the *Fleur de la Mort*.

Fleur de Jour.

Fleur le Beau.

Fleur de la Lune.

FLEUR DE LA MORT!

Billy grabbed the scroll that was marked

with the name of Laura's ship and stashed it in his pocket. He started to run out of the records room, but a name written on a scroll lying open upon the table caught his eye: Jack Sparrow. Hadn't Arabella just been talking about him? The paper said something about Sparrow's being wanted for a list of numerous crimes. One was tricking a six-year-old boy into masquerading as an officer of the Crown. Billy furrowed his brow. What type of man was this Jack Sparrow, anyway?

Billy moved the scroll. Beneath it he found something else that interested him: his own arrest report and criminal record. He smiled, rolled up both records, and took them with him.

The sounds of battle still raged at the other end of the ship. Billy had just emerged from the records room when suddenly the entire ship began to list to one side. There was no way that anything happening in the battle could have caused the boat to sway so much. The ship was practically on its side. Billy clung to the railing, doing his best to keep himself aboard.

Just before it seemed as though the ship would tip completely over, it began to straighten itself out. But as soon as it was right-side up, the ship continued to list and began to dip dramatically toward the *other* side. Screams were coming now from the opposite end of the ship. Billy could hear splashing, and he knew that some who were aboard must have been thrown off. He hoped that Arabella and Jean were not among them. He needed to deliver the stolen record to them; it was the only way he could repay them for risking their own lives by setting him free.

As suddenly as it had tipped, the ship

began to straighten out again. Billy was prepared for yet another roll, but this time the ship just swayed back and forth. Looking over the railing, Billy saw by the pale moonlight a vast, slithering shape moving across the water. Its long, wide body glided just below the surface of the sea. It was like a whale, but ten times as long.

Confused, not to mention a bit worried, Billy rushed back to the fore end of the ship. It was still rocking to and fro significantly. Billy noticed that either most of the navy sailors were too stunned to continue fighting, or they had already been beaten by Laura and her crew.

"Come on!" Laura shouted, jumping off the deck into the darkness and disappearing back to wherever she had come from. The boy with the obsidian blade was right behind her. Then Jean, who held the disgusting cat tightly in his arms, followed. With a leap off the ship, each of them was gone.

"Arabella! Now!" Laura's voice rang from out in the pitch-black night.

Arabella stood on the railing, looking around hesitantly. Billy called out to her. Their eyes met, and he saw that although she still looked at him skeptically, she seemed a bit more sympathetic now. She lifted her head and jumped into the night to join the rest of her crew.

"Avast! Halt there!" a voice called out.

It was the admiral, and Billy immediately knew he was speaking to him.

He gasped as the admiral drew his sword and began to run toward him. Billy leaped up on the railing of the ship. The admiral swiped at Billy with his sword, but Billy nimbly jumped up at every swipe, avoiding his blade by mere inches.

"Billy!" a voice suddenly called out from behind him.

It was Arabella.

"Jump!" she cried. "Jump now!"

Billy looked behind him. There was nothing but dark, open sea and a coal black night sky. He turned, and there was a madman wielding his sword. Billy did the only thing he could. He turned around again, and against all logic or reasoning, jumped.

CHAPTER SEVEN

$\mathcal{B}$illy looked around. He was completely disoriented. He had landed on the deck of a huge, beautiful French warship. All around him, the members of the pirate crew, which he had been fighting alongside on the Royal Navy vessel, were steadying themselves and attempting to get their composure back. Arabella had one arm braced on a mast and was breathing heavily, trying to regain her strength, which seemed to have been exhausted during the battle.

Billy turned around and saw that they were already sailing quickly away from the navy vessel they had all just fought on. He looked back at the deck of the ship he had landed on. Where had it come from? How could it be that he hadn't been able to see it when he was aboard the navy vessel? Could the sailors on that ship see him now? Did they know he had escaped to a pirate ship and was sailing away with the crew? He figured not. The ship had not been visible to him while *he* was on the navy vessel, so it probably was not visible to anyone who was not aboard it.

So, now he knew where the out-of-thin-air pirates had come from. But it didn't explain how a ship could render itself and its crew invisible. It also didn't explain where the giant creature that caused the navy boat to list had come from. Could the pirates have summoned it?

"What was that thing?" the Mayan-looking sailor asked, as though to prove Billy's thoughts wrong.

"It looked like some kind of sea beast. Something from Davy Jones's Locker . . . perhaps the Kraken itself . . ." Arabella said between heavy breaths.

"Oh, daughter, must you always be so dramatic? If it were the Kraken we'd have been torn asunder," Laura responded. She, too, seemed exhausted, but she was hiding it better than the others were.

"Well, whatever it was, I'm glad it decided to swim by when it did. It certainly tipped the scales in our favor," Jean put in.

Suddenly, Laura looked at Billy and sneered. She walked over to him and pointed her sword at his chin. "What's this, and what is it doing aboard my ship?" she asked. Her expression was severe. It was clear she meant business, and Billy felt a tremor of fear run through him. He looked at Arabella, who lowered her eyes.

Laura sighed. "Please tell me you didn't—oh, you're such a fool. You can't take every handsome man with soulful eyes aboard."

"It's *not* like that, Mother!" Arabella said simply.

"Oh, then, do tell what it *is* like, exactly," Laura responded, sneering again.

"He was going to *help* us," Jean said, stepping in to defend Arabella.

"Keep quiet!" Laura said.

"Yes, ma'am!" Jean snapped back to attention and quickly shut up.

"First of all, 'going to help us' does not mean that he actually has. In fact, he is almost certainly a liability. Do you think the navy hasn't enough reason to come searching for us? Do you think they needed one more act of treason to pin upon us? Further, how is it that you can be so sure that he is not a navy agent himself? You might've just brought the enemy aboard. Children, children, children . . . You've all so much to learn about pirating." Laura paused, sighing condescendingly, and the crew hung their heads.

She walked over to Billy again and patted his cheek lightly. "Besides, he might be pretty, but he does not look very intelligent."

Billy scowled. He was usually very even-tempered, but he had never been one to take an insult without responding.

"Not intelligent, ma'am?" Billy snapped. A few crewmembers inhaled sharply. Jean gestured to indicate that Billy should not antagonize Laura. But it was too late. Her face was red with rage, and she put her hand on the hilt of her sword at her hip. Arabella gasped.

Billy grabbed for something at his hip as well. And then the captain and Billy both drew. . . .

Laura stood with her sword lifted high over her head. But Billy hadn't drawn a sword. He had pulled out an entirely different sort of weapon.

It was the scroll that he had taken from the naval ship's records room.

"What's this?" Laura asked warily, lowering her sword.

"Open it and see for yourself," Billy said, handing Laura the scroll. His hand was shaking with a mix of terror and rage.

Laura stowed her sword and took the item. She unrolled it and examined it closely. Her scowl quickly re-formed into a broad smile.

She cocked her head to one side and threw open her arms.

"Come here, mate!" Laura said.

Billy was taken aback by Laura's sudden shift in mood, but the expressions on the faces of the crew seemed to suggest that he should just play along as she threw her arms around him and hugged him tightly.

"Welcome to the crew of the *Fleur de la Mort*. I always knew you could be trusted. It was just the judgment of this bratty crew that made me second-guess my faith in you. I'm Captain Laura Smith. I believe you've already met my beautiful, if dim, daughter, Arabella, and her Creole companion, Jean. The fellow with the shiny black knife over there is Tumen, and the nasty little feline that Jean is holding is called Constance. Jean insists that she's his sister, under some sort of mystical spell, but none of us really knows for sure. We can't believe that anyone who was once human could be quite *that* nasty."

Constance hissed and jumped from Jean's arms, retreating to a dark corner of the deck.

"And you are . . . ?" Laura asked, calmer now, though her voice still held a hint of condescension.

"Billy, ma'am. Billy Turner."

"Mum, what does the record say? Where are they holding Mr. Reece?" Arabella asked, jumping between them. She placed her hand on her mother's arm and peered over her shoulder at the scroll.

"Port Royal, of course. We should have known. They intend to execute him along with a group of five other pirates in a week's time. In fact, Billy Turner, it looks as though you were meant to be the final member of this morbid and offensive act," Laura said.

Billy felt a lump form in his throat. It

seemed so strange that pirates, whom he had always thought of as the scourges of the seas, should be his salvation. An hour earlier, as a prisoner aboard the navy vessel, he had had almost no hope of surviving the month. And now, he was a free man, surrounded by a group who seemed more than capable of protecting him.

Laura gave Billy one last pat on the shoulder, then began to walk toward the ship's wheel, barking orders at the crew.

"Tumen, set our course for Port Royal! Jean, ready the ship and keep that rat-cat thing of yours away from me! We've not much time. The trip to Port Royal can take as long as a week. We'll need to catch some good wind if we're to make it there before Mr. Reece's execution."

Laura looked at her daughter and smiled weakly.

"Arabella, Billy Turner, make yourselves useful," Laura said.

"What would ye like us to do, Mum?" Arabella asked.

"You're a big girl, figure it out," Laura said, waving her hand airily as she stomped away.

"Look, I'm sorry for the way I treated ye," Arabella said to Billy when they were alone.

"No, don't be. I understand. I would have acted the same way. I was a prisoner aboard a government vessel. Truth be told, I'm not sure I would have set me free if I were in your position. So, thank you," Billy said.

A short but very uncomfortable silence followed. Billy took the opportunity to find out more about the ship.

"So, would you mind telling me why it was that I couldn't see this huge ship from the navy vessel?" he asked.

"The *Fleur's* sails are charmed. Made from

special thread or something, Mum says, though I'm not quite sure that even she knows how it works. She told me the boat already had the ability to cloak itself when she—er—acquired it from its previous captain. Anyway, regardless of why or how they work, when the sails are unfurled, the ship and anything on it becomes invisible to anyone who's not aboard."

Billy couldn't help laughing.

"That's the most ridiculous thing I've ever heard!"

"Any more ridiculous than the giant sea beast we all saw tip that large navy ship?" Arabella asked.

Billy shrugged.

"Thought not," Arabella said smugly.

"It has to work some other way. There has to be some explanation, through science or logic. Mirrors or something . . ." Billy persisted.

"Billy, I'm sure ye've seen some strange

things these past few weeks at sea. I wish I could tell ye that I had all the answers or that things would become less strange over time, but that'd be a lie. Since I've been sailing on the Caribbean, I've seen things I don't think I'll ever be able to explain if I live to be a hundred. Yer going t'see more of it, and if ye want to survive, if ye want to keep yerself *sane*, take my advice, and don't try to ask yerself too many questions about how and why . . . just accept that whatever is, *is*."

Billy wasn't entirely comfortable with this way of thinking. It had always been in his nature to try to figure things out. Simply accepting the idea that a ship could turn invisible seemed foolhardy to him. In fact, the more he thought about it, the more uncomfortable he became.

Instead of dwelling on this, he decided to change the subject. "So where exactly are we headed now? I mean, I know we're sailing to Port Royal, but once we get there . . ." he asked.

"Mum's first mate, Mr. Reece, was taken prisoner by the Royal Navy shortly after we left port in New Orleans. He's about the only person in the world me mum has any type of allegiance toward, so we're going to break him out," Arabella explained.

"Rescuing two government prisoners in as many weeks?" Billy asked.

Arabella shrugged and sighed.

"I'm not happy about it. But once ye decide to live the life of a pirate—well, let's just say that the freedom of being at sea— well, it comes with a price."

After his experiences aboard the *Sea Star* and the navy ship, the trip to Port Royal almost seemed relaxing. That's not to say that Billy didn't pull his weight aboard the boat. He did. But it was certainly less stressful than being under the constant scrutiny of Mr. Hawk, or being locked up in a dirty pen in the brig.

When they finally docked in Port Royal, Billy couldn't deny he was frightened by what was in store for him. After all, the navy would be there, executing other people who were accused of being pirates. This is where *he* would have been executed.

Over the week, Billy had begun to feel that it was his duty to free those other people. If he were innocent, couldn't it be true that the others might be as well? And even if they were pirates . . . well, the pirates he encountered had treated him better than anyone else he'd met at sea.

This gave him the strength to pick himself up by his bootstraps and follow the crew off the *Fleur* to the execution. Through an associate named Mr. Gibbs, Laura had secured navy uniforms for the crew to wear to help them blend in. Gibbs, Billy learned, was a member of the navy, but acted only in his own best interests, which often meant that he helped pirates.

Arabella had her hair pulled back in a ponytail, copying a style many men wore. For the first time Billy was struck by just how beautiful her face was. Her feminine charm shone through in spite of her tomboyishness.

Once they were suited up and armed, the crew joined the crowd gathered in Port Royal's square. It was just before noon. Glancing around, Laura sneered. Clearly, she was uncomfortable and out of place in such a "respectable" town.

"There he is!" Arabella whispered to Billy.

Billy saw a tall, muscular, handsome man—who seemed unusually clean for a pirate—

walking toward the scaffold. As he walked past the crew, Laura caught his eye, and he smiled knowingly. The other prisoners were already on the scaffold, where they were to be hanged.

"Arabella, Jean, stay here and guard the way out. Billy, Tumen, make your way behind the scaffold," Laura whispered.

Arabella nodded nervously as Laura weaved through the crowd toward the front of the scaffold. As directed, Billy and Tumen headed behind the scaffold, where a group of officers had gathered.

A hush came over the noisy crowd as Mr. Reece approached the scaffold. A tall officer in an ivory colored wig cleared his throat and read Mr. Reece the charges against him. Billy could hardly believe one man could have committed so many crimes. And some of them were downright odd—such as "crossing a canal with a swine aboard his vessel in order to bring ill luck upon the Crown."

Once the charges were read, Mr. Reece was taken by his bound arms and helped up onto the platform.

At that moment, Laura jumped up behind him, tossed off her officer's hat, and severed her first mate's bonds. The speed with which she operated made Billy dizzy. Everything seemed a complete blur.

Laura tossed Mr. Reece a sword.

"Were you nervous?" Laura asked Mr. Reece.

"Not for a moment," he responded.

The crowd erupted into a panic, and people began running everywhere. Screams of "Pirates!" rose up from the square.

Tumen turned to Billy. "Come on!" he cried. Billy watched Tumen carefully as he leaped up onto the scaffold and cut the other condemned pirates' bonds with his obsidian blade. Billy and Tumen armed the freed pirates, and a melee broke out in the square.

All Billy could hear was the clanking of swords. He had never used a sword before, and the weapon felt awkward in his hand.

"Billy, look out!" Tumen shouted.

Billy's eyes widened as a sword came down right next to him, missing his ear by mere inches. Doing his best to look threatening while handling a weapon he didn't know how to use, he watched as the rest of the crew fought with the officers. He soon discovered that he had a talent for evading his opponent's swipes, though his offense was weak.

"To the *Fleur!*" Laura commanded after what felt like ages.

Billy managed to make his way next to Arabella.

"How on earth is she going to find an invisible ship in the harbor?" Billy asked.

"She's got a compass that points to it!" Arabella replied.

Billy was not going to question what seemed to be yet one more ridiculous detail. Instead he watched Arabella as she expertly maneuvered her sword, fending off as many officers as she could. He felt very safe next to her.

"What are ye waiting for, Billy? Ye heard Mum . . . to the *Fleur*! Now!"

Billy noticed that Jean, Tumen, and Mr. Reece were already running behind Laura, making their way to the ship. But Arabella was still fighting.

Suddenly he realized that she was fighting to keep *him* safe.

"Go!" she shouted.

Billy took off and followed the others. He could hear Arabella's footsteps right behind him. He followed the crew to the harbor and once again watched as they appeared to vanish into thin air while actually boarding the invisible ship. He and Arabella were feet from where the ship must have been docked when Billy heard a loud scream.

He turned around to see Arabella pinned to the ground under the boot of a huge navy officer. The man was at least a full head taller than Billy. His sword was raised over his head, and it was clear that in seconds it was going to come down on Arabella.

Without hesitating, Billy jumped forward and raised his own sword. He sliced at the officer's forearm, causing the huge man to howl in agony, dropping his weapon. Billy caught the officer's sword and held both weapons up threateningly.

"Get off of her. Now!" Billy said.

"Not on your life, pirate," the officer replied.

"Fine, then," Billy said. "It'll be on *yours*."

Billy swiped at the officer's legs with his swords, cutting them severely. The man screamed in pain and fell away from Arabella.

Billy pulled her to her feet.

"Y-ye saved me life," Arabella stuttered.

"Come on," Billy said.

They ran to the invisible ship, judging where it must have been docked based on where they had last seen the rest of the crew. Billy held Arabella tight, then jumped onto the gangplank, rendering himself and Arabella invisible to their pursuers. As soon as they were aboard, the gangplank was raised and the lines that held the ship at bay cut.

They were out to sea again. And they were safe . . . for now.

CHAPTER EIGHT

The feeling of safety didn't last long. Billy felt something warm and wet on his leg. Looking down, he saw that he was bleeding badly. In the chaos of the battle, he hadn't even noticed that he'd been cut. Still, it was a wonder that that was all that had happened to him. He was an untrained swordsman and had been thrown into a conflict with the Royal Navy. It could have been much worse.

"Yer bleeding!" Arabella gasped.

"I'll heal," Billy responded, limping toward a mast to lean against.

Billy teetered a bit; Arabella rushed over to help him. She took his arm and threw it over her shoulder.

"Ye need some support, Billy."

Billy grimaced, trying to hide the pain. But this was becoming more difficult, especially as some of the blood began to dry and crack around his wound.

"I've got some medical provisions in my cabin," Arabella said.

Billy nodded and, with her help, hobbled over to Arabella's cabin. It was very tidy for a pirate's room, with a neat little cot in a corner beneath the only window; a writing desk; a large chest; and nothing else. Arabella sat Billy down on the cot, which was quickly stained with his blood. She helped him put his feet up and then went over to the chest and opened it. She rummaged through some things and finally returned with some cloths.

"Jean!" she called. "Can ye fetch me a jug of saltwater?"

Arabella set out the cloths as Jean delivered the jug.

"Anything else, *Mademoiselle*?" he asked, smiling.

Arabella shot Jean an expression that Billy hadn't yet seen her exhibit. It was clear she wanted Jean to leave, but there was a playfulness about it, too. It was nice to see her not so serious.

"Right, then," Jean said. "Feel better, Billy."

Before the young sailor closed the door, he winked at Billy and smiled. Billy shifted uncomfortably, both from the pain and the awkwardness of being alone in a room with a girl.

"I'm not gonna hurt ye," Arabella said, smiling.

That didn't make Billy feel any better.

Arabella grabbed a knife from the chest, and Billy jerked back.

"It's fer yer pants, ye dolt," Arabella said as she pulled Billy's trouser leg tight enough to cut through it. With the fabric gone, the wound was revealed. It was deeper than Billy had thought, though it didn't appear to have gone through to the bone.

Arabella pulled out a basin from beneath her cot. She lifted Billy's leg over it. Then she grabbed the pitcher that Jean had delivered, and Billy's eyes widened. He began to shake his head, but before he could protest, Arabella had poured the saltwater over his wound. It felt as though she'd poured a gallon of fire over his throbbing leg. He let out an undignified yelp.

"Oh, hush," Arabella said. "It'll not only clean yer wound, but the salt will help heal ye up."

It felt as if all the blood in Billy's body had rushed to his wound and was pulsing around it. Arabella quickly grabbed a cloth and tightly wrapped his leg. Billy could see some blood seeping through the cloth, but after a while the blood stopped spreading, and the throbbing started to settle down.

"Thank you," Billy said, gritting his teeth.

"Yer welcome," Arabella said, smiling. She pushed him off the sheets and collected them. "Ye know, I'm sorry fer not being so nice to ye when we first met. It's just, well, have ye seen me mum? I thought the woman was dead up till a few months ago. I once watched as another pirate pulled her from our tavern by the hair, with a sword in his hands.* Of course

* Arabella recounts this story in Vol. 3, *The Pirate Chase*.

I expected the worst. Who wouldn't? Me dad became a drunk after we lost her, and I ran away from home. I went to sail the seas with Jack Sparrow, who ye've heard a little about, and who d'ye think I bump into on the high seas but mum? It was hard to accept that she was alive, and a pirate, no less. It's not very easy being the daughter of a pirate. Not very easy to trust people when that's yer background . . .

"Ye seem like a nice fellow. Not like the kind t'come from pirates," Arabella went on, as she soaked and wrung out the sheets that had become soiled with blood.

"I wouldn't know if my parents were pirates or cobblers," Billy said. "I never knew them. They disappeared when I was an infant."

"What a pity," Arabella said, "not to know yer parents."

From outside the cabin, Billy could hear

Laura barking orders. He cocked one eyebrow quizzically at Arabella. With a mother like that, could she really be serious?

"Tumen, we're not sailing quickly enough! Catch a better wind! Jean, get that darned cat away from me! Arabella! Where in Davy Jones's Locker are you, girl?"

"Best be going," Arabella said. She looked thoughtfully at Billy. Then she smiled, leaned over, and kissed him on the forehead. Billy flushed.

"Rest here," she said as she opened the cabin door to leave.

From outside, Billy heard Laura snapping at Arabella.

"Arabella, what were you doing lolly-gagging around? Are you not aware that I have a ship to run? You never listen. Never have. I should . . . What? Don't brush me off, young lady!"

Billy smiled and leaned back on the cot. He detected a salty-sweet scent on the thin pillow. It was the same one that he'd caught every time Arabella passed him by. It relaxed him, bringing him a state of comfort that he hadn't experienced since this whole crazy adventure had started.

The *Fleur* was swaying gently, rocking Billy to sleep. As the rocking continued, Billy fell further and further into a deeper sleep. He dreamed of the Isle of Man and of North Carolina; of Crumbs and Aunt Erin and Uncle Seamus; he dreamed of Jack and what he might be like—he pictured him as a dashingly handsome, clean-cut sailor wearing a spotless, heroic captain's outfit; and he dreamed of Arabella.

Suddenly, it felt as if the boat had been pulled out from under him.

He woke with a start, his heart in throat.

When he opened his eyes, he saw that the room was on its side. Arabella's little bit of furniture had shifted. Her trunk was open and its contents were sprawled on the floor.

Just as quickly as it had lurched to one side, the ship straightened itself out. Then it tipped violently to the other side. The entire sequence of events felt eerily familiar to Billy, who struggled to his feet. A scream came from outside the cabin. It was Arabella.

Billy managed to maintain his balance. His leg was throbbing, but he ignored the burning pain. He grabbed a sword from Arabella's trunk and bolted out of the room.

He didn't get far. What he saw caused him to come to a dead stop. Just beyond the deck, the hugest, most vile, most wretched beast Billy had ever seen swayed over the ship. Its long, limbless body looked like a huge serpent. It had two fins beneath its jaw, which was filled with rows of foot-long fangs.

Arabella had fallen to the deck right beneath the beast. She was looking up at it, trembling. Its huge, pinkish form swayed to and fro as it attempted to hold itself erect over the ship. Foamy blue saliva dripped from its gaping maw and sizzled as it fell to the deck. It was like nothing Billy had ever seen before.

Or had he seen it before? The tipping of the ship, the fin on its back. Billy was beginning to put the pieces together. This was the beast he had seen when he was on the *Star*, surrounded by dead sea creatures.

Billy's thoughts were interrupted by the appearance of Laura at his side.

"Can it see us?" Billy shouted.

"I don't know, and I'm not sure it matters," she replied. Then she rushed over and pulled Arabella up as the ship continued to rock. "It seems it's able to do enough damage to the ship whether we're invisible to it or not."

The beast reared back, and the crew, which had all gathered on the deck, recoiled. Something that sounded like thunder rumbled from the beast's belly. Its face turned a bright reddish purple, and a visible lump made its way up to its throat. The beast seemed to breathe in, and then, with a great hacking sound, spat all over the ship. Bits of chewed fish, entire shark carcasses, broken crabs, jagged shells, and chunks of coral rained down on the crew. The bits were covered in viscous goo, which stank like vomit.

"Ugh!" Arabella cried as she shook a rotting, half-digested octopus from her arm.

Billy blinked to clear his eyes of the filmy goo, then noticed a piece of wood beside him. If it weren't for the bright paint, it wouldn't have stood out among the other flotsam and jetsam with which the beast had spattered the deck. Billy noticed a partial word, *Ane* . . . painted on the wood. It looked familiar. He picked up the piece of wood and wiped off some of the slime. *Anemone.*

His skiff.

This beast, which he'd seen so often since he'd left the Isle of Man, had devoured his skiff. Could it have had the ability to completely deplete the waters around the Isle of Man of sea life? Billy looked up at its gaping jaws, which looked powerful enough to empty the Atlantic, and his question was answered.

With a roar, Billy rushed to the broadside of the ship, where the beast was still hovering. As he approached, the beast growled fiercely and snapped at him. Billy leaped away, favoring his good leg, just barely escaping the beast's jaws. But he didn't escape its tail. The beast used it to wrap itself around Billy.

Raising his sword, Billy slashed at the tail, causing the beast to let go. He fell to the deck. Behind him he heard the others gasp.

"Billy!" Arabella screamed.

He stood and began to approach the creature again. "It's the reason my family's starving," Billy cried over his shoulder. "It's the reason I'm out here at sea, and that I've been arrested and called a pirate. It's the reason I spent a night in a filthy holding cell and was forced to commit acts of treason!"

"Billy, what are you on about?" Arabella said.

"Darling, I hope you weren't interested in this lad. He seems a bit, well, odd—even for you," Laura said.

Billy moved toward the beast.

"Billy, stop!" Arabella called out to him. "I've seen beasts like this before!"*

"You have?" Laura said, taken aback.

Arabella ignored her.

"You need to get it in the heart," Arabella continued.

"That won't be too difficult," Billy said, plunging his sword into the beast's midsection, which was directly in front of him. The beast howled as the wound gushed bluish blood.

Billy smiled. But the beast reared back again, furious.

"No, Billy! Their hearts are located right under their jaws."

Billy's eyes widened as he looked at the beast's open mouth. He quickly unwrapped

---

* Arabella encountered a beast like this in Vol. 2, *The Siren Song*.

his bandages. They were still damp with fresh blood. He sneered and began to wave them in front of the beast.

"If he's anything like a shark," Billy said, "he'll smell this up there." Billy motioned to the beast's head, which was a good twenty feet above him.

Sure enough, the beast dived toward the deck, snapping at the bloody bandages. It managed to slurp one up with its forked tongue, just missing Billy's hand. Then it reassumed its position above the deck.

Billy continued to wave his bandages, and the beast dived again. This time, just as it descended, Billy grabbed the fin right under the creature's jaw. The beast twitched violently, and Billy was tossed about like a rag doll. Billy managed to brace the foot of his good leg against the broadside and steady himself. This gave him a little more power over the beast, but he knew he didn't have much time.

Using the sword he had only just begun to learn to wield, he slipped it in cleanly below the beast's jaw. He prayed that he'd hit the right spot. A moment later, blue blood issued forth, and he was sure he had hit it in the heart.

The beast jerked back over the ship and writhed around, spraying its blood all over the charmed sails of the *Fleur de la Mort*. The crew ran for cover, but Billy stayed put right under it.

Finally, after what felt like eons, the beast crashed to the deck. Its head landed right in front of Billy, while its enormous body hung over the side of the ship, extending into the sea.

Arabella ran to Billy's side and threw her arms around him. Despite the horror of the moment, Billy couldn't help but think it felt nice.

Laura walked up to the beast and kicked it in the jaw.

"I appreciate your valor, Mr. Turner," she said. "But now, if you'd be so kind, get this gruesome *thing* off my ship."

"Yes, sir, er . . . ma'am," Billy replied.

But Laura didn't notice his stammering.

The captain's eyebrows were knit, and her expression looked fiercer than it had at any point during the short time Billy had known her. At first he thought she might be angry with him for some reason. But he quickly realized that she was looking *past* him. Billy had his back to the sea, so he didn't know immediately what it was that had Laura and the whole crew of the *Fleur* in fact, frozen in a state of shock, anger, and panic.

"Oh, me stars," Arabella said. Her mouth

dropped open in what was a nearly blank expression of terror and awe.

Billy whirled around. And what he saw alongside the *Fleur* caused him to blanch with fear and boil with rage, all at once.

CHAPTER NINE

"*R*eady the cannons!" Laura shouted.

Mr. Reece, Jean, and Tumen scrambled, preparing for battle. Arabella dragged sacks of gunpowder to the guns as the men readied them.

Billy found that he could not move. A sea beast was one thing. This was worse.

On the horizon, barely a league away and quickly gaining on the *Fleur*, was the *Sea Star*.

"Ready!" Laura shouted, lifting her cutlass high above her head. Billy knew that as soon as Laura brought the cutlass down, the cannons would explode and the *Sea Star* would be gone forever—with luck. If not, she was right on track to crash into—and destroy—the *Fleur*.

As their ship came within a mile of the other, Billy began to make out figures moving about the deck. Mr. Hawk and Captain Donovan would be among them. He knew they couldn't see the *Fleur* with its sails unfurled. The cannons would fire, and the *Sea Star* would never know what hit it. No matter how angry Billy was at the crew, this thought moved and terrified him.

"Aim!" Laura shouted.

The *Sea Star* continued to move closer. Billy grabbed Tumen's spyglass and looked through it to read the name painted on the hull. He thought about how the crew had sold him out to the navy in order to roam free themselves. He remembered how afraid he had been before he had boarded the ship and become part of its crew, and he remembered how Mr. Hawk had helped him to learn about the ship and understand the crew.

"Fi—" Laura began. But Billy grabbed her arm before she could signal and shouted, "No!"

The crew halted their preparations and stared at Billy. They turned toward Laura, who looked as if she might explode. Wearily, they turned back to Billy. Then they turned to Laura again.

"Your mother had better be on that ship, boy," she said through gritted teeth.

"Pardon, ma'am?" Billy asked.

"That is about the only excuse I *might*

grant you for what you've done."

Billy hung his head. When he looked up again he saw Arabella running over to her mother.

"Mum!" she cried, "cut the man some slack. After all, he saved me life . . . twice!"

"I wouldn't care if he'd saved my *own* life *ten* times, daughter. He's interfered with my execution of a vendetta that's been raging for years now between the *Fleur* and the *Sea Star*. That cannot be forgiven. It's in—"

"—the code. Yes, I know," Arabella finished. "Funny how you pirates invoke that blasted code only when it's convenient."

"Er, speaking of the *Sea Star*," Mr. Reece said, "has anyone noticed how close it is to us?"

Laura spat and cursed. Billy's eyes bulged. The *Sea Star* was now perhaps a half mile away. The *Fleur* would never be able to get

139

out of the *Star*'s path in time. It would be a miracle if the two ships avoided each other.

"We only have one option. Furl the main-sail," Laura said, glaring at Billy.

"Furl?" Mr. Reece said. "Captain, we're already at a disadvantage. Furling the sail will make us visible. Is it wise to do so? And further, a furled sail will prevent us from catching any wind. We are doomed to Davy Jones's Locker already. If we—"

"*Do not question me,*" Laura said, and by Mr. Reece's expression, Billy could tell that Laura had rarely, if ever, blown up at Mr. Reece.

"Aye, ma'am," he replied, and he hurried along with the rest of the crew to raise the mainsail.

Once it was secured, shouts and murmurs could be heard from the approaching ship as the *Fleur* became visible, only a few hundred feet now lying between the two vessels. Billy could see the sails shifting, as every man on the deck of the *Star* seemed to be attempting to turn the great ship around.

"What a way for it all to end, *non*?" Jean asked. "All these adventures with Jack and aboard the *Fleur*, and we get sideswiped by a ship that couldn't see us."

Tumen nodded.

"I can't look," Arabella said, covering her eyes.

Billy put his arm around her and pulled her close. She buried her head in his chest. Billy closed his eyes tightly and pressed his face against the top of her head. He remembered smelling her hair on her pillow not even an hour before. It's funny, he thought, the things you ponder right before you breathe your last breath.

The screams from the approaching ship

grew closer and closer. And then, a crash—the grinding and snapping of metal and wood—and the entire *Fleur* began to rock almost as severely as it had when it was attacked by the sea beast.

Billy opened his eyes and pushed Arabella behind him. He was not going to die like this. He was going to get himself, and the crew, off the ship. And then he realized something. The *Sea Star* hadn't crashed into them head on! It had managed to turn enough so that the broadsides smashed into each other. Billy was sure the ships would still have endured some damage, but it was possible that it wasn't so great.

Billy's brief moment of relief ended when he realized that the *Sea Star* was close enough to the *Fleur* to attack. Both decks were about the same height, and before any member of the *Fleur*'s crew could react, the crew of the *Sea Star* were jumping aboard, waving their weapons above their heads.

"Take no prisoners, but take the *Fleur*! Imagine! She can travel between worlds! Where else could it have been coming from to appear so suddenly before us?" Billy heard Captain Donovan yell. "Only Davy Jones's cursed *Flying Dutchman* is known to do such things. The crew aboard owe us in kind, as they slaughtered our pet beast! That beast that we once used to leech the seas of its fruits until men deserted their homes, possessions, even entire islands so that we could move in and acquire what was once theirs. But we will have no need for that monster any longer. We will have no need for meager deserted towns. With this ship, we will *rule* the Caribbean!"

"Pet beast?" Billy said. Could it be? Could the *Sea Star* have been controlling the vile monster that swallowed all the fish from around the Isle of Man? That meant that the *Sea Star* was responsible not only for landing Billy in prison, but also for forcing him to leave his home in the first place.

"Pirates!" Laura cried to the other ship's men. "The *Fleur* has been pursuing you for three years now, since you captured the loot that was ours by right after we defeated the renegade pirate Left-Foot Louis!"

"Pirates?" Billy said, not sure he could handle any further surprises.

So the *Sea Star* wasn't a merchant vessel at all. Billy had been thrown in a filthy brig and branded a pirate by the navy when he might have been the only honest man aboard the ship!

Billy felt something inside him that he had never felt before. It was as if all the anxieties he had had since boarding the *Star* had finally boiled over. But instead of being afraid of these feelings, Billy harnessed them into a power that he never knew he had within him. He ran to Laura's side, swiped a sword from her waist, and ran, screaming like a berserker, toward the crew of the *Sea Star*.

The crew charged him. And the *Fleur*'s crew charged them back.

"This is more like it," Laura said, smiling.

Billy began swiftly slashing away at the *Star*'s crew. The sword felt natural in his hand . . . as if he'd been using one all his life. He pointed it at one sailor's chest and the sailor fell overboard, between the *Star* and the *Fleur*. This method of disposing with enemy sailors met with a lot of success, and Billy managed to send a good portion of the *Star*'s crew over the broadside, one after another, while carefully watching his own steps to assure that he did not wind up among the waves with them.

Behind him, the rest of the *Fleur*'s crew was fighting ferociously. Arabella looked like an expert swordswoman, Jean and Tumen made a great team, and Constance— well, of all the crewmembers, Billy thought she might be the most brutal. The cat looked at him and hissed, and he quivered before quickly turning his attention back to the fight.

"Four men remaining!" Arabella shouted. "Plus the captain and his mate!"

Billy looked over. Sure enough, Captain Donovan and Mr. Hawk were holding their own against the crew of the *Fleur*. This was unacceptable to Billy, and he ran over to battle them. But the remaining crewmembers ambushed him, and Billy was forced to spar with all four at once.

"Billy!" Arabella shouted.

She ran to him and began dueling with two of the four rival pirates. Jean and Tumen soon joined them, and the odds were once again even. Meanwhile, Laura was battling Captain Donovan, and Mr. Reece was sparring with Mr. Hawk.

Tumen ducked quickly and sliced a pirate's leg with his obsidian blade. The pirate howled in pain, and Tumen pushed him over the balustrade. He winced as the pirate splashed into the sea.

The pirate who was battling with Jean was caught off guard by his crewmate's fall from the ship. When he pulled his attention away from the young sailor, Jean quickly took advantage by poking him in the backside with his sword, forcing him to join his companion in the waters below.

Meanwhile, Billy and Arabella were

backed up against the *Fleur*'s railing, slicing for their lives with their swords. They both had their backs to the railing and couldn't lean back any farther to avoid the returning swipes without running the risk of toppling overboard.

"How are ye doing?" Arabella asked, out of breath.

"Oh, fine," Billy replied, attempting to sound confident.

"Bear with me here, will ye?" Arabella said.

"Er—sure," Billy answered.

Before he knew exactly what was happening, Arabella leaned forward, kneed both men, and, as they keeled over quickly, looped behind them.

"Toss them, now!" she shouted.

And without any hesitation, Billy planted a boot firmly on each of the pirates, jettisoning them from the ship. He and Arabella looked over the side, watching as the men splashed into the water, only to bob up again and begin struggling back to the *Star*. Looking at each other, Billy and Arabella smiled.

"Ahoy! Battle's not over yet!" Mr. Reece called out. He sounded desperate. The captain and the cook were not letting up.

A streak of black shot across the deck and wove its way among the *Sea Star* pirates' legs. Whatever it was, it caused the two men to topple over. The *Fleur*'s crew rushed over, and all six members leaned over the captain and the cook, pointing their swords at them.

"Constance!" Jean said happily. "You did it again, *belle!*"

Constance was sitting on top of Captain Donovan, purring. She had been the black blur that caused the men to topple.

Laura was breathing heavily. "Have you—

anything—to—say—for—yourselves—before—
we toss—you—over?" she asked between
gasps of air.

Billy put up a hand.

"No. These men have no right to speak,"
Billy said. "But I do." He glared down at the
two men whom he had trusted at one time,
not very long ago at all.

"You lied to me," Billy said. "You tricked
me, and when it was convenient, you turned
me over, though I'd wronged neither you nor
the Crown in any way. You made me believe
you cared for me—that I had a great deal to
learn from you. You and that beast tore me
from my home, my family—my Crumbs . . ."

"Well, I hardly think crumbs are anything
to complain about losing . . ." Laura mumbled.

"Captain Smith," Billy continued, too
angry to process Laura's comment, "I say
that tossing these men over the broadside is

too good a fate for them. Of course, they might be devoured by sharks, or Davy Jones might come for them. But they also might escape back to the *Star*. I propose that we deliver them to the very thing that they were creating with their treacherous beast—a desert island where the chance of rescue is slim to none and where they will be forced to live out the rest of their days knowing only each other for company and companionship."

A sinister smile spread across Laura's face. It was clear she liked the idea.

She liked it a lot.

CHAPTER TEN

Billy felt little remorse as the *Fleur* sailed away and Captain Donovan and Mr. Hawk grew smaller on the horizon. Captain Smith had scouted the first desert island they could find. She wanted to make sure there was just enough food and clean water available there. She thought their misery should last as long as possible.

Billy thought Laura was a very cruel woman, but he didn't argue.

Despite Billy's ambivalence about the fate of the crew from the *Sea Star*, he did feel something else stirring within him—a sense of belonging. After all these years, Billy had finally discovered what made him happy: sailing freely over swells and whitecaps; high adventure on the high seas. Sure, it was a dangerous life, but didn't Arabella say that freedom always came at a price?

And Billy soon learned that the price was often high. In the first six months during which he sailed with Captain Smith, he was kidnapped by a vicious breed of creature called the merfolk, had to evade the East India Trading Company twice, helped defeat a powerful storm king, uncovered a plot to steal the very stone that controls the tides, and, finally, met and became crewmates with the famous Captain Jack Sparrow, whom he had heard so much about.*

And Billy was able to do something else in the half year that passed. . . .

On a mid-April morning, months after he had first set sail on the *Sea Star*, Billy and Arabella docked a small boat, which Jack Sparrow had "secured" for them, off a calm, sandy beach. Early spring smells of honeysuckle and thawing earth were all around, and the air had that pleasant and mild feel that brought to mind a soft, light sweater.

Billy stepped off the boat first and looked around. Arabella followed.

"Are ye sure this is the place?" Arabella asked.

"Certain," Billy said, smiling.

* Some of these adventures are recounted in Jack Sparrow Vols. 11 and 12, *Poseidon's Peak* and *Bold New Horizons*. The other tales are yet to be told. . . .

"That's what ye've said the past three times we docked, Billy."

Billy didn't answer. There was someone . . . some*thing* . . . running toward him from the far end of the beach. Billy smiled and began to run to meet it.

"Crumbs, boy!" Billy said, starting to squat down to pet the dog that ran to meet him. Crumbs knocked Billy to the ground and pinned him there. He licked his face ferociously.

"So this is yer pup, eh?" Arabella said through a smirk.

"Yes, ma'am!" Billy said, sliding out from under Crumbs, who began to run circles around him.

Arabella patted the dog on its haunches.

"Pleased to meet ye. I've heard a lot about ye!"

Crumbs licked Arabella's hand fiercely

and then barked, encouraging Billy to follow him.

"I'm coming, Crumbs! I'm coming!"

The dog led Billy and Arabella up the beach and past some dunes to a quaint little cottage, which was handsome and well built. Billy looked at Arabella, who smiled and nodded. He took a deep breath and opened the door, stepping into a neat and cozy living quarters.

Aunt Erin looked up from her knitting. Her eyes widened and her mouth fell open. Her lip quivered.

"B—Billy!"

She rushed over to Billy and threw her arms around him.

"Billy!" Another voice boomed through the room—it was Uncle Seamus's. "Welcome to North Carolina!"

Billy had never in his life felt more at

home or at peace. He beamed as he looked around the cottage. A pot of something that smelled rich and tasty was boiling on the hearth. The room was sparsely but tastefully furnished.

"Oh, Billy," Aunt Erin said, "when we sent you off aboard that ship, we were scared to death. We had no idea if we had done the right thing or what would happen to you." She looked at Uncle Seamus and nodded. "But in the end, it was the right thing to do."

"I'd never believed the stories that here in America you could make so much money so quickly. But look at you! Look at *us*! And all this, just by basket weaving . . . it's truly amazing," Uncle Seamus said.

Arabella and Billy gave each other a nervous glance. They weren't sure that Billy's aunt and uncle would believe the lie they'd come up with, that Billy had amassed a fortune weaving baskets. In truth, Laura Smith had apportioned an allotment of the *Fleur*'s treasure to Billy in return for service aboard the ship. Billy knew that he could never tell his aunt or uncle that. It might kill them to think they were living off pirate loot. They knew nothing of what had transpired aboard the *Sea Star*, and Billy swore that they never would.

"Um, Aunt Erin, Uncle Seamus, this is Arabella. Arabella, this is Aunt Erin and Uncle Seamus," Billy said, steering the conversation away from his "profession."

"A fine career and a beautiful lass to boot!" Uncle Seamus said. "We should have sent you over here ages ago."

Billy smiled awkwardly.

"No, it's not like that. She's a friend. Well, a coworker. I mean, I work with her mum, aboard a ship. That is, her mum transports my baskets . . ."

"No need to explain, Billy," Aunt Erin said, winking at Arabella. "Come darling, I'll show you how to knit booties. I'm making some for Crumbs right now. The winters are surprisingly chilly here in North Carolina."

"Thank you, Aunt Erin. But, knitting's not really me thing. I'll just . . ."

"Oh, nonsense, knitting is every girl's thing!"

Billy smiled wryly as Aunt Erin led her away. He saw her mouth the words *help me* as she was pulled into the sitting room. Billy just shrugged and laughed.

A few hours later, Arabella had knitted her very first pair of booties, which looked more like lopsided coin purses, and Billy had hiked the beach twice with Uncle Seamus and Crumbs. And then it was time to go.

Billy's heart sank. He wanted to stay for days, weeks, maybe forever.

But if he were to keep his aunt and uncle, and Crumbs, living so comfortably, he'd need to get back aboard the *Fleur* and report for duty.

"Why the Caribbean, lad? Why couldn't you just set up your basket shop here in North Carolina?" Uncle Seamus said.

"It's just how it happened. The island of Barbuda is known for its basket weaving. It's the place to be if you're a basket weaver," Billy said.

"I didn't know that," Uncle Seamus said.

"Neither did I, until I met that group of basket weavers aboard the *Sea Star* what taught me, er, basket-weavey things."

"Promise to visit us again soon," Uncle Seamus said.

"I will."

"And promise to bring me some baskets next time you do," Aunt Erin said. "I could use some of those miniature ones for my berries."

Billy suppressed a laugh. "I will."

Crumbs rushed to Billy's side and licked his hand. The dog began to howl.

"Don't worry, boy, I'll be back. Soon. I promise," Billy said, kissing the dog's head. He was pleased to see how much weight Crumbs had gained. He could hardly feel the dog's ribs as he patted his side.

Arabella and Billy waved good-bye and made their way down the beach and back toward the boat. Billy was barely able to hold back his tears.

"Ye know," Arabella said, "I wonder what it'd be like."

"What's that?" Billy asked.

"No pirate mother, no half-crazed captains like Jack to bark orders at ye. No invisible ships or Pirate Codes. Maybe just a little seaside cottage to relax in."

Billy smiled coyly. He looked down at the crude booties she was holding in her hands.

"Oh, and while you're at it, a baby, too, then?" Billy said, laughing.

"Sure, why not?" Arabella said. "A boy."

"Well, I'm not sure that's the type of life for people like us. We're pirates, after all, lass."

"Yeah, I guess you're right. Still, it's nice to think about it, isn't it?"

"Yes," Billy said. "Yes, it is."

He took Arabella's hand and they walked down the beach toward their boat. The surf was getting rough, and the waves beat violently against the boat—they were the kind of waves that could either help a boat speed along, or warn of a terrible coming storm.

THE END

And now for the Other Stories . . . The following five tales are rare stories of the young Jack Sparrow and his crew. Some are deleted scenes from books you might have read ("The Bedeviled Egg" from *The Age of Bronze*, "Not-So-Calm Before the Storm" from *The Coming Storm*), and others first appeared in magazines or on Web sites. They are re-presented together here for the first time.

Tale One

Not-So-Calm Before the Storm

*J*ack Sparrow was having a difficult night. He'd arrived on the outskirts of the rough-and-tumble town of Tortuga a short time ago, thirsty and hungry. Hoisting the sack that contained his few personal belongings up onto his shoulder, he walked toward the docks. He approached the first person he saw, a disheveled man of questionable sanity who was lying near a gutter mumbling to himself.

"Say, where can a mate find food in this town?" Jack asked, leaning down.

"What?" the man yelled.

"Food," Jack said. "Edibles. Stew, rice, condiments, that sort of thing."

"What?" the man yelled again, squinting. The man leaned in so close that Jack could smell the foul stench of his breath.

"Oh, never mind. You're obviously useless. Or out of your gourd. Probably both," Jack said, walking away.

"Psst! You there!" a voice behind him called out.

"Sir," Jack began, not turning around, "I will not indulge you, as I know full well that if I respond you will simply scream 'what' in my ear and infiltrate my nostrils with your putrid odor. So, as they say in New Orleans, scat, cat. Savvy?"

A firm hand suddenly landed on Jack's

shoulder, stopping him in his tracks.

"You looking for a bite to eat, boy?"

Jack turned to face his pursuer. It was not the man he had left in the gutter after all, but a huge sailor who wore a sword on either hip. "Try the Faithful Bride inn. The bread is stale and the meat all stringy, but it's the only place for food around these parts. Of course, the company you'll be keeping will be, well, questionable. All old salts and dock hands—even pirates," the man said, winking at Jack.

"Thank you, sir," Jack said, relieved. "Now if you can direct me . . ."

"First, I require payment."

"Oh, are you the innkeeper in question? What a novel way to solicit customers, sneaking up behind them and—"

"No! The payment is for advising you," the man said.

"All I can offer you is my thanks, I'm afraid. See, this bag here is all I have," Jack explained.

"That'll do!" the man responded, ripping the sack from Jack's shoulder.

"Oh, no, you don't, mate," Jack said. He lunged for the sailor, who ducked quickly out of the way. But Jack was quicker. He managed to grab one of the sailor's swords, and they began to spar. Jack jumped onto the dock, and their fencing continued up and down the pier.

A storm was approaching, and the surf below them roared and crashed. Ships moored just off the shore were rocking in the wind like toy boats. The sailor took a swipe at Jack and knocked the sword from his hand. The sword flew into the water, and when the sailor glanced over at it, Jack managed to knock him into the water, too.

"Score one for Jack Sparrow," Jack said. Then he realized that the bag had fallen in the water with him. He looked down into the rough water, but there was no sign of the sailor—or his bag. Then, at the other end of the dock, Jack Sparrow spotted the dripping-wet rogue running off toward town.

"Now, how on earth did you do that, mate?" Jack said.

He had no idea how a man could get from one place to another so quickly, but he did have an idea where a man like his adversary might be headed—a place where any pirate could find safety in numbers—the Faithful Bride.

Tale Two

The Nosy Stranger

*T*eenage stowaway Jack Sparrow gazed out at the open sea and smiled. Only hours ago, he had been at the mercy of a coven of nasty mermaids—the merfolk, as they called themselves—who were holding his crew hostage. He'd escaped from the merfolk and saved his crew, and now they were on their way to securing one of the Caribbean's greatest treasures—the magical Sword of Cortés!

At least Jack *thought* they were well on their way. That was, until his tiny boat—the *Barnacle*—hit a snag.

"Whoa!" Jack shouted, grabbing on to a mast. The crew was thrown forward as the ship came to an abrupt halt.

"Tumen! Jean!" Jack called out to two of his crewmates angrily. "Did anyone ask you to drop anchor? And by anyone, I mean me, myself, or I. Savvy?"

The two young sailors just shrugged.

"We're not anchored, Jack," Jean said.

"Then we must have hit a reef," Jack surmised. "Survey this ship, at once!" he barked.

"Um, Jack, pardon the wee interruption," Jack's first mate, Arabella, chimed in, "but it seems like we're not stuck in a reef at all. Unless reefs breathe and move around."

Jack's eyes nearly popped out of his head

as he looked overboard. The *Barnacle* was stuck right in the side of . . . something. And that something was clearly alive! The creature began to squirm. And before the crew could even think about reacting, the monster had reared itself up, hurling the *Barnacle* back into the water.

"What is that thing?" Fitzwilliam P. Dalton III, Jack's aristocratic crewmate asked, regaining his composure and drawing his sword.

"Beats me, chap," Jack responded.

As the beast rose up from the water, there seemed to be no end to it. Nor was there any real shape to it. It was just a moving blob. And it just kept rising and rising from the water.

Jean ran to Constance—a cat Jean claimed was really his sister, under a mystic's curse— and gathered her up in his arms. He was clearly shaken as the rising beast now completely blocked the sun, casting the small boat into shadow.

Arabella turned to Fitzwilliam. "You'd best put that sword away," she said to him. "Were ye to use it on this monster, it would have no more effect than a pin sticking ye."

"He is rather large," Jack said in a flat tone. "Of course, that means he has a large nose somewhere."

"What?" Fitzwilliam said condescendingly. "Of what possible consequence could *that* be?"

Jack winked at Fitzwilliam and smiled. Then Jack began to pace back and forth on the deck. He scanned the huge beast, looking for any place where the beast's face could possibly be on the squirming blob. Then, quite suddenly, the face emerged right in front of him. Its terrible eyes and mouth took up the whole length of the *Barnacle*. And its terrible nose did, too!

Jack smiled and drew his sword.

"Jack! I told ye, a sword will not do a thing to this beast!" Arabella shouted.

Jack stopped short at the broadside, leaned over, reached with his sword toward the beast's nose, and began to rub the sword over its nostrils, ever so gently. The beast opened its mouth wider and wider as the crew ran belowdecks in terror. Then, suddenly, a great roar issued from the beast, followed by an unearthly gust of wind. The wind caught in the *Barnacle*'s sails, propelling it out into the sea and far away from the beast.

"No idea a boat could travel so fast," Jack said. "I like it!" He smiled.

When the boat finally slowed, the crew emerged from belowdecks. The deck, and Jack, were covered in sticky green slime. The sun was shining again. And, most important, there was no sea monster to be found.

"This slime is disgusting," Fitzwilliam proclaimed, careful not to get any on himself.

"And it smells," Jean said.

"Where did it come from? Where is that wretched creature?" Arabella asked.

Jack just smiled and wiped his slime-covered hands on his pants.

"Never mind," he said, marveling at how messy a sea monster's sneeze could actually be. "Suffice it to say that the threat has past. And now . . . let us continue our course to Isla Fortuna! There's a magical sword there with my—er—*our* name on it!"

Tale Three

The Bedeviled Egg

*J*ack Sparrow and his crew were tired and hungry. They'd arrived in the city of New Orleans a short time ago, and the first thing that Jack wanted to do was find a place where he could have a good meal.

"Well, I don't know about the rest of you mates, but *I* for one, have an angry little monster what lives in my tummy, and right now he's growling quite loudly for chow," Jack said to his crew.

Jack's first mate, Arabella Smith, glared at Jack disapprovingly.

"We're *all* famished, Jack," she said, "but first things first. We're here to find the mysterious mystic Madame Minuit. And ye know it won't be easy! We've been told she can hide in plain sight, after all."

Fitzwilliam P. Dalton III, an aristocrat-turned-crewmate, nodded in agreement. "And her pet snakes are said to be able to throw a person into a dizzy trance," Fitzwilliam added.

"So, even if we *do* find her, it'll be not so easy to pin her down," Tumen, a Mayan crewmember, said.

"Then it's settled," Arabella stated. "We find Madame Minuit before we do anything else."

Jack twitched with irritation. Then he cleared his throat and stood bolt upright.

"Only *three* people make decisions around here—me, myself, and *I* . . . savvy?"

"I have to agree with Jack, Arabella," said Jean Magliore, another member of the crew who, up till then, had remained silent. He was petting his cat, Constance—who he claimed was his *human* sister, enchanted by a mystic's curse. Jack smiled smugly and nodded approvingly at Jean. "After all, our captain is *fou* enough when he is not starving. Can you imagine how much lack of food might increase his insanity?"

Jack's satisfied expression quickly faded. "If my own crew will not give me respect, then I will be on my way. Enjoy the city. Hope you survive! Though that's doubtful without me around," he mumbled as he stormed off and into the dark alleys of the Crescent City.

The streets were littered with heaps of

trash, and a thick smell of days-old meat hung in the air.

Jack made his way down a narrow path called Pirates' Alley. He was not surprised that the tiny road was true to its name. New Orleans had a reputation for piracy that was surpassed only by the pirate town of Tortuga, where Jack had met Arabella. A half dozen men and one woman were lounging lazily in the alleyway. They all wore telltale signs of the pirate's life. None looked as though he or she had bathed in weeks. Their fingers were adorned with gaudy rings, and some had beads dangling from their hair. Some of the men wore makeup on their eyes.

Jack walked over to one of the men. The pirate was hugging a barrel of something and dozing off. His pleasant expression contrasted with his otherwise intimidating appearance. Jack decided the pirate must be drunk on whatever it was that was in that barrel.

"Excuse me, mate," Jack said merrily.

The pirate just brushed him off, clearly too much at ease to be bothered with dirty little children.

"Well, sorry, then, didn't intend to disturb your inebriation" Jack said indignantly. "Can't a mate just find something to eat around here?" Jack asked.

The filthy woman at the dark end of the alley jumped up eagerly.

"Fond of eggs much?" she asked.

"Fond of just about anything at this point," Jack said, sizing her up.

"A gold piece," the woman demanded, thrusting her open palm before him.

Jack grimaced, dug into his coat pocket, and dropped a gold coin into her hand.

She smiled, revealing a mouthful of rotten

teeth. She reached into her own jacket and pulled out a perfectly round egg.

"What kind of chicken laid *that*?" Jack said, sneering in disapproval.

"If you're not hungry, I'll happily take it back," the woman replied.

"No, no, no," Jack said, taking the egg from her. Its shell was soft, and the liquid inside made it feel especially squishy. Jack hesitated for a moment and then popped it into his mouth.

He squinted as he chewed. A thick, slimy substance squirted from the egg.

"Mmm, not too bad," Jack said. "Then again, nothing is really that bad when you're as hungry as . . ."

Jack stopped in midsentence. Suddenly, the world began to transform itself. The alley seemed to fade into obscurity. Swirling lights appeared around Jack. Before him, under a beaded veil, appeared one of the most beautiful women he had ever seen. She stepped forward, and Jack was so taken by her that he couldn't utter a word. She reached a hand toward him, and a long green snake began to slither down her arm. This woman was clearly Madame Minuit! Jack needed to get back to his crew to tell them he'd found her.

But he couldn't move. Madame Minuit's snake came face to face with him and hissed violently. The snaked reared back, ready to strike. It spat wildly, and then, just before it sank its teeth into his cheek, Jack shuddered and looked around. Everything was back to normal. The lights were gone, and so was the beautiful woman. Standing in her place was the hideous pirate who had given him the egg.

"What in the Seven Seas was that thing you gave me?" Jack asked her.

"An egg."

"I am no dolt, and that was no egg," Jack said flatly.

"Oh, it was," the pirate woman replied. "It was the best type of egg—one that nourishes you with a glimpse into your future." She laughed evilly.

"If that was my future, I'd elect to stay in the present. Except for the pretty-lady part. I'd like her to be in my future. Can we arrange that?" Jack said.

The woman spat at Jack and called to the other pirates to follow her out of the alley.

As the seconds passed, Jack remembered less and less of the vision that had come to him. He tried hard to remember what he'd seen when he was under the spell of the egg, but it was no use. He could barely make out the image of a woman. He remembered there being an animal involved, but he couldn't remember which kind. He didn't have time to think about it now. He needed to get back to his crew. They were on a quest to find the vicious pirate queen of New Orleans . . . the dreaded Madame Minuit. And if his crew was right, she'd be very difficult to find.

Tale Four

The Mermaid Key

Jack Sparrow sighed. He and the crew aboard what Jack believed to be his mighty ship, the *Barnacle* (in truth it was little more than a damaged old fishing boat), were in desperate need of freshwater. And Jack could not find an island—with or without potable water—anywhere. Looking out over the *Barnacle*'s rail, all Jack saw was the turquoise Caribbean Sea and an occasional bird.

"Well, this is quite the predicament, isn't

it?" he said, turning to Arabella, his first mate. "If we are to continue sailing the seas freely, we will need water, but if there is no water to be had, there is no crew to sail and then sailing the seas freely is not an option, savvy?"

Arabella nodded at Jack's confusing logic. "Yer right, Jack. What would ye like us to do, 'Captain'? Conjure up an island from thin air?" she asked sarcastically.

Jack opened his mouth to reply to his first mate's snotty tone—after all, he *was* the captain! He deserved some respect! But then, something portside caught his eye. Squinting, he looked harder. Then a smug smile crept across his face.

"None of us might be able to conjure an island willy-nilly, Bell, but I, as in me, *moi*, *yo*, etcetera, as usual, have found us our salvation. Look." Jack pointed over the rail and watched as Arabella's eyes widened.

Not far away was an island. True, it was small. But it was an island nonetheless. "Make fast to port," Jack ordered.

A short while later, the *Barnacle* sailed up to a rather decrepit dock. As the rest of the crew set off in search of water, Jack took to the gravelly roads that indicated that this island was settled. It had been a while since he'd had any excitement, and he was eager to search some out.

He didn't have to look for long. He had barely set foot on dry land when the air filled with a most unpleasant odor—like a combination of honey and rotting fish. Jack crinkled his nose and looked around, only then turning slowly to look behind him, where he noticed the stench thickening. He found himself face to face with a man who looked as awful as the smell that was wafting from him.

The old fisherman's coat was ragged and worn through with holes, and his hair hung in clumps off his balding head. When he walked toward Jack, his water-filled boots made a sloshing sound.

"You be looking for something?" the man asked, revealing two rows of brown teeth as he spoke.

"Aye," Jack replied, moving a step back and waving the air in front of his nose to vanquish the smell. "See, mate, me and my crew have just made a small side trip here to this lovely island of yours in search of water." The old man lifted his elbow and scratched his underarm. Jack was nearly overcome by the smell.

Nearly fainting, he continued, "Perhaps you can show me the way? Take a dip in the fine, *clean* water, wash off that . . . smell . . . you got there? What say ye?"

The man ignored Jack's advice and stepped closer. "You be needing something. And I be having it." As he spoke, the man reached into his pocket and pulled out a key. It was old and tarnished and attached to a piece of twine. Holding it toward Jack, the man added, "Take this and be wise to the ways of the sea. This is a powerful key. Do not let the ladies have it." He dropped it in Jack's open palm.

Jack looked down.

"Yes, very well," Jack said, casually pocketing the key. "But if you'll recall that story I told you, not so long ago—and by that I mean maybe a minute or two earlier than the present time—it's water I need. Not some rusty, moldy, *stinky* key."

The man did not respond. He looked a bit perturbed. "If you don't want it, give it back," he said.

The strange man lunged for Jack, clearly

feeling wronged. Jack squealed and jumped out of his way, but before the fight could go any further, the air filled with a loud buzzing noise. Jack's eyes grew wide, and the old man's eyes filled with terror.

"They've found me," he cried. "They've found me!" And before Jack could even ask who, the old man ran off, leaving a very confused Jack in his wake.

But Jack wasn't confused for long. Looking over his shoulder, he saw just what had found the fisherman—a swarm of killer bees! And they were coming right toward Jack. With yet another screech, he took off toward the *Barnacle*, his arms flailing in every direction.

The rest of Jack's crew had returned to the ship and were waiting with freshwater. Looking over the rail, they saw their fearless captain skipping quite swiftly and panickingly toward them, trailed closely by a large black swarm of winged danger.

"What kind of trouble has Jack found now?" Fitzwilliam P. Dalton III, the *Barnacle*'s resident aristocrat swashbuckler, asked.

"No time for questions, Fitzy," Jack shouted breathlessly as he jumped on board. "Swarm of bees. Back. Behind me. Smelly man. Yucky key. Leave now!"

The crew looked confused. Jack looked frustrated.

"Set sail!" Jack clarified. "Or we're all to become the buzzing beasties' midday snack."

As the rest of the crew leaped into action, Constance, the mangy feline which Jean Magliore claimed was his enchanted sister, began to hiss. Ignoring her, Jack waved his sword in the air.

"Stay back, you pests!" he commanded the angry swarm.

Behind Jack, Constance's hisses grew louder and louder. Then, just as the bees reached the dock, Constance let out one long, incredibly feral-sounding hiss. The crew had never heard her do this before, and they seemed a bit jarred by it. Even the bees appeared to stop in midswarm. Then, just as quickly as they had appeared, they disappeared.

Looking over at Constance, Jack cocked his head. "I always thought that hiss of yours was particularly loathsome. Glad to see it finally did some good."

Ignoring Jean's glare, Jack turned to the rest of the crew.

"It seems I have come into possession of something that makes stingy little creatures and stinky men go mad."

He held up the key.

"Jack—do ye even know what that key might open?" Arabella asked.

"Not clear to me at present, no. But I'm Jack Sparrow. It is bound to come to me sooner or later."

Sometime toward the later end of things, Jack was attempting to use the key to open something—anything he could find. Knots in wood, cracks in the deck, Constance's ear . . . but try as he might, there was nothing he could make it fit into. He was so preoccupied by his task that he didn't notice that the rest of his crew had grown eerily silent.

"Blasted key!" he shouted as he jammed his thumb—again—trying to open a small box he had found among Fitzwilliam's effects. He was about to ask that another of his crew offer up an item to be opened when he realized that his crew would be of no help. Arabella, Fitzwilliam, Jean, and Jean's best friend, Tumen, were all standing at the rail, looking down at the water, completely entranced.

Jack knew that look. He had seen it before, specifically the last time he and the crew had come across the nasty merfolk and their song. It made everyone who heard it go a bit, well, sleepylike. Jack sighed. Perhaps it was good he hadn't bothered to clean his ears in a while. And even if he hadn't, it wouldn't have mattered much. Jack had discovered during his very first encounter with the merfolk that their song had no effect on him. The song forced you to try to obtain your heart's desire, usually leading you to ruin. But because Jack's heart's desire was to be free, he couldn't be trapped by the melody, which would have enslaved him.

"Seems the Scaly Tails are back for a visit," Jack said, matter-of-factly.

He walked over to the railing and followed

his crew's gaze into the sea. Not a Scaly Tail, as Jack called the merfolk, in sight. Then the water began to bubble and roll, as if it were boiling. Within moments, hundreds of mermaids appeared.

"Ladies! To what do I owe the privilege of your company?" Jack asked. "Did you miss me?"

A proud and hard voice spoke up: "We do not miss things, as you do, human. And we especially feel nothing for the likes of you."

Looking through the crowd of mermaids, Jack spotted the familiar red hair of Morveren, one of the mermaid leaders. Her eyes were cold as the deep sea as she stared at Jack. He had a feeling that Morveren had taken a liking to him. So, Jack winked at her.

"Jack Sparrow, you are a loathsome creature," Morveren hissed.

Oh, well, Jack thought, *been wrong before*.

"You have something of ours," Morveren said. "To unlock the sea is not your duty nor your right."

"Pardon me, fishy lady, but I'm not aware of any of this rights-duty business," Jack replied, clutching the key tightly now. When the old man had handed him the key, he had mentioned "ladies." Could he have meant these Scaly Tails?

A moment later, Jack had his answer.

"Do not fool with us again, Jack!" Morveren hissed, her forked tongue flapping. "You have the key, and it is not yours to have! Give it over to us and we will free your crew. A fair deal, we feel."

The sharp teeth of hundreds of merfolk chattered in agreement.

"Now, why would I go and do a foolish thing like that?" Jack asked. "It's peaceful with the crew all quietlike and starry-eyed. I was getting a bit tired of Fitzy's constant blabbering to be honest."

"Enough!" Morveren shouted. "You will hand over the key now!"

"Not likely, Scaly Tail. You can try, but as I recall from our last few meetings, I always seem to best you folk," Jack said smugly.

For a moment, Morveren did not speak. Then, with a subtle nod to her army, she dived under the water and disappeared. As the last glimpse of her red hair and blue tail disappeared into the deep, Jack's crew began to stir and wake.

"See that, mates?" he said, puffing up his chest. "Those Scaly Tails are all fish and no guts."

But he had spoken too soon. With a creak of timber, the *Barnacle* began to rock back and forth atop the water. Looking down, Jack let out a cry. The merfolk were pushing his ship! Harder and harder they pushed, causing the ship to rock faster and faster. Reaching out, Jack grabbed the rail and tried to steady himself, as all around him, his crew fell to the deck. The *Barnacle* jolted forward one final time and nearly tipped over completely. Before Jack knew what was happening, the key flew out of his hand and high into the air. He watched in horror as the key arced into the sky, glinting in the sun. Then, with a plunk, it dropped into the water and began to sink— straight into the waiting hands of a Scaly Tail.

Immediately, the rocking stopped and the mermaids vanished.

Jack sighed.

"Well, the key is gone," Jack said.

"Does it really matter?" Jean asked, when his head had cleared. "We didn't know what it would have opened anyway, so have we really lost anything at all?"

This train of thought was too philosophical, even for Jack, who was used to complex logic.

"Though the merfolk would have only been protecting something of value," Arabella put in. She thrust a canteen into Jack's hand, and he slumped, bewildered, onto the deck. Constance strutted by, hissing at Jack for no apparent reason, and he hissed back. He'd give this key business some thought. After all, he was sure he'd be seeing the Scaly Tails again. For now, however, all he needed was a nice, cold drink.

"This here canteen feels a little bit light," Jack said, puzzled.

The crew looked at the deck guiltily.

"We were *really* thirsty," Tumen said.

Jack walked over to the *Barnacle*'s railing. Maybe jumping into the sea wasn't such a bad idea after all.

Tale Five

The Cat's Meow

"*J*ack!" Jean called out from the stern of the *Barnacle*. The young sailor held fast to the mizzenmast for support as the rough sea rocked the boat fiercely. "Jack, I can't find my sister! I can't find Constance!"

Jean had been a crewmember on Captain Jack Sparrow's boat, the *Barnacle*—which was little more than a beat-up old fishing vessel—for just over two weeks now. He'd met the young captain when Jack and his crew had rescued him, along with Jean's best friend, a Mayan sailor named Tumen, from the island on which they had been shipwrecked.

When the crew of the *Barnacle* disembarked on Isla Esquelética in the hopes of finding water, food, and shelter, they'd found a whole lot more: a crumbling kingdom, hidden treasure, and a powerfully cursed pirate captain. They'd also found Jean and Tumen, and—most unfortunately, as far as Jack was concerned—Constance.

"Jack," Jean continued, holding a line as he made his way over to his captain, who stood on the forecastle, "she was here just a moment ago, and now I can't find her anywhere. You know how she hates the sea. You know she's no good near water."

"Then a boat is a fine place for her, isn't it?" Jack quipped.

"*Mon ami*, this is serious. Don't you remember what happened the last time we couldn't find her?"

"How could I forget?" Jack replied. "Especially as it was little more than two hours ago."

Jean shook his head in frustration. "She had gotten into the stores of fish we had belowdecks. She had no way of knowing that they had gone bad. . . ."

Jack was in the process of fastening some rigging and did not take his attention away from his work as he replied. "Sorry they hadn't gone 'worse,'" he said in a flat voice.

"Jack, she *died!*" Jean said, shocked by Jack's callousness.

"And yet she is somehow *still* roaming the deck of this boat," Jack said, still not looking up from the rigging.

"Jack, what do you have against my dear

sister?" Jean asked. "What has Constance ever done to you?"

"Well, let's see. The time before she got into the spoiled fish, she fell overboard while chasing a bilge rat. That was preceded by a climb up to—and, subsequently, a nasty fall from—the mainmast. At our last port, I recall a nasty run-in with a butcher's cleaver when she tried to steal some fresh meat, a dangerously fatal game of hopscotch in which she was trampled, and a severe allergic reaction when she mistook coconut nectar for the milk of a cow."

"Don't ye go forgetting the time she was trapped in the treasure chest for three days," Jack's first mate, Arabella, piped up from the bow.

"Yes, there was that, too," Jack said.

Jean shook his head somberly. "And each of those times . . ."

"She passed on," Jack finished for him. "Yes, a true pity. Sadder still that she keeps coming back to rear her ugly—and I do mean ugly—head."

"Jack," Arabella said, "let's be fair now. Don't ye think yer being the slightest bit *insensitive*?"

"The thought never crossed my mind," Jack said.

Just then, the faint sound of a cat's mewing wafted over the deck.

"Constance!" Jean shouted, "Constance, where are you, *ma soeur*?"

"Unfortunately, it seems, not gone for good," Jack muttered, still not taking his attention away from the lines he was securing.

"Jack!" Arabella said, slapping Jack's arm in a reprimand, but clearly holding back her laughter.

"What I would like to know is what kind

of 'sister' goes around mewing like a cat," Jack said.

"One who has been *turned into* a cat by the mystic Tia Dalma, that's what kind of sister," Jean responded indignantly.

"Okay, I have had just about enough of this," Jack said impatiently, finally turning his face to Jean. "Since we rescued you, your friend Tumen, and this mangy cat-beast that you have always *claimed* is your sister, all I have been hearing is 'my dear Constance' this and 'my dear sister' that. Let me now go on record as saying that no matter what fantastic things I have seen on our voyages, I do not believe that that cat is your sibling."

"And why not?" Jean asked, stamping his foot.

"Because I do not believe any mystic such as Tia Dalma would knowingly create something so nasty, awful, and—I hate to tell you—smelly as that mangy thing hanging off the bowsprit."

"Hanging off the bow—" Jean said. And then: "Constance!"

Jean looked out at the edge of the bowsprit, to which Constance was clinging for dear life. Jean was too frightened to move.

"Oh, Jack, we must save her. Please!"

Jack looked up and sighed. "Why bother?" he asked. "If she falls off she'll only come back moments later, hissing and scratching at us all."

"But, you don't understand," Jean started. "The fish, the rat, the mast, the cleaver, the nasty game of hopscotch, the coconut nectar, her time in the treasure chest . . . Jack, a cat only has nine lives. My poor sister has already gone through seven. She only has two lives left!"

"Actually," Arabella said, stepping forward,

now noticeably concerned, "she only has *one* life left. Yer forgetting that time she got a wee bit too close to that jaguar in Costa Rica."

Sheer panic gripped Jean. He could not move. "Jack, please, do something!"

"Okay. I will do something. Yes, I know *exactly* what I'll do," Jack said. "I'll just let her fall into the ocean and hope Arabella hasn't miscounted how many lives she has left."

Jean was now sweating profusely and shaking wildly. He darted toward the bowsprit, ready to attempt to save Constance, but it was clear he was in no shape to do any rescuing.

Jack grabbed Jean by the arm. "Wait right here, mate," he said, rolling his eyes. Then he jumped up onto the bowsprit, crawled up the length, grabbed Constance by the scruff of the neck, and carried her safely back on board. He jumped down onto the deck and planted Constance down next to Jean.

"You owe me," Jack said, wiping his hands and returning to the rigging.

"Oh, *mon ami, mon ami!*" Jean said, near tears. "*How* can I ever repay you?"

"How about keeping that fleabag off my cot from now on?" Jack said.

Constance glared up at Jack and her fur stiffened. Then she batted at Jack's boot, her claws bared, tearing at the leather. She spat for good measure, then sauntered away to the other end of the *Barnacle*.

Jack sneered at Jean. He didn't need to say a word.

"Ummm," Jean began uncomfortably, "well, I think I'll be going now. Down belowdecks. Best be getting out of your hair, Jack. Sparrow. I mean, *Captain. Captain* Jack Sparrow."

Jean darted away from Jack, and Jack quickly leaped after him, setting off a chase that would perhaps last hours, given Jean's nimble agility.

Arabella just smiled and looked over the broadside toward the horizon. She was happy to be there, on the adventure of a lifetime, with a crew whose company she enjoyed so deeply. The sun had begun to set, turning the sky shades of every color. She took in a deep breath: the fresh salt air, the comforting smell of the dry deck, and then, suddenly, the horrible stench of something wet, moldy, and rancid. She looked down to see Constance rubbing against her leg—a limp rat in it's mouth.

Arabella's face turned bright red. "Jean!" she cried out. "Ye'd best pray yer sister here isn't the only one with nine lives!" Then she darted off to join Jack in chasing down the young salt as the *Barnacle* sailed of into the sunset and deeper into the world of intrigue and adventure that awaited.

And now, meet the young

PIRATES *of the* **CARIBBEAN**

and their greatest
adversaries. . . .

Jack Sparrow

First appearance:
(as Young Jack Sparrow):
Jack Sparrow, Vol.1: *The Coming Storm*

Known relatives:
Teague (suspected father); Captain Ace Brannigan (uncle); Quick Draw McFlemming (aunt); "Grandmama" (paternal grandmother)

Nickname:
Jackie

Sails aboard:
Barnacle, *Grand Barnacle*, *Fleur de la Mort*

History:
Jack Sparrow ran away from home and from the man who might be his father, Teague, who was Keeper of the Pirate Code. His original intention was to forsake his family and their pirating ways. But after Jack secured a "ship" (really a boat) called the *Barnacle* and assembled his first crew, he found himself involuntarily pulled into the world of seafaring and pirating. Taking a break from captaining, young Jack currently sails aboard the *Fleur de la Mort* under Captain Laura Smith.

Key stories:
Jack Sparrow, Vol. 1: *The Coming Storm*; Jack Sparrow, Vol. 10: *Sins of the Father*; Jack Sparrow, Vol. 12: *Bold New Horizons*

Arabella Smith

First appearance:
Jack Sparrow, Vol. 1: *The Coming Storm*

Known relative:
Captain Laura Smith (mother)

Nicknames:
Bella, Bell

Sails aboard:
Barnacle; *Fleur de la Mort*

History:
Arabella was a barmaid at the Faithful Bride, an inn and tavern frequented by the Caribbean's fiercest pirates. On the night she met Jack Sparrow, he convinced her to leave the tavern behind and follow him on a quest for freedom, adventure, and a very special sword that would grant the wielder unimaginable power—the Sword of Cortés. During her adventures with Jack, Arabella was reunited with her mother, who up till that point Arabella had believed to be dead. She eventually left Jack's crew to sail with her mother, the pirate captain Laura Smith, aboard her mother's ship, the *Fleur de la Mort*. As fate would have it, Arabella and Jack were reunited some months later and once again became crewmates—this time, aboard the *Fleur*.

Key stories:
Jack Sparrow, Vol. 1: *The Coming Storm*; Jack Sparrow, Vol. 3: *The Pirate Chase*; Jack Sparrow, Vol. 6: *Silver*

Bill Turner

First appearance
(as Young Billy Turner):
Jack Sparrow, Vol. 11: *Poseidon's Peak*

Known relatives:
Erin Haskins (maternal aunt); Seamus Haskins (uncle)

Nicknames:
Bloody Billy; Billy

Sails aboard:
Fleur de la Mort; *Sea Star*

History:
Billy Turner was a fisherman on the Isle of Man. He was in the care of his aunt and uncle, but when the sea around the island went mysteriously empty, they could not afford to keep him and sent him away to America. Along the way Billy encountered some high adventure— and a pirate crew or two. By the time he'd reached America, his experiences had turned him into a bona fide pirate.

Key story:
Jack Sparrow Super Special Vol. 1: *The Tale of Billy Turner and Other Stories*

Fitzwilliam P. Dalton III

First appearance:
Jack Sparrow, Vol 1: *The Coming Storm*

Known relatives:
James Norrington (cousin); Admiral Norrington (uncle)

Nicknames:
Fitzy; Fitz

Weapons and special items:
a pocket watch that can warp time

Sails aboard:
Barnacle; any number of Company and navy ships

History:
Fitzwilliam P. Dalton III was a spy for the Royal Navy and the East India Trading Company. He managed to join Jack Sparrow's crew in an attempt to locate Teague, Jack's father and the Keeper of the Pirate Code. Jack spent most of his first year at sea with Fitzwilliam, and when the rest of his crew left him to join the *Fleur*, Fitzwilliam was the sole crewmember to stay aboard the *Barnacle*. This was not a decision he made out of loyalty to Jack, but as a way to continue spying on him. Fitzwilliam is currently once again operating with the Royal Navy.

Key story:
Jack Sparrow, Vol. 10: *Sins of the Father*

Jean Magliore

First appearance:
Jack Sparrow, Vol 1: *The Coming Storm*

Known relative:
Constance Magliore (sister)

Sails aboard:
Barnacle; *Fleur de la Mort*

Weapons and special items:
ring of skeleton keys

History:
Jean Magliore is a Creole sailor. He, his sister, Constance, and his mate Tumen, were the sole survivors of a shipwreck upon Isla Esquelética, where they were rescued by Jack Sparrow and the crew of the *Barnacle*. Jean soon joined the *Barnacle*'s crew. He loves good food, particularly the gumbo sold in New Orleans.

Key stories:
Jack Sparrow, Vol. 1, *The Coming Storm*; Legends of the Brethren Court, Vol. 1: *The Caribbean*

Tumen

First appearance:
Jack Sparrow, Vol 1: *The Coming Storm*

Known relatives:
Mam (great-grandfather); Kan (brother); K'ay (sister); Chila (brother)

Sails aboard:
Barnacle; *Fleur de la Mort*

Weapons and special items:
obsidian knife

History:
Tumen was kidnapped and sold to a merchant ship when he was very young. He met his best friend, Jean, and Jean's sister, Constance, while working on the ship. The three were rescued by the *Barnacle* after a hurricane caused by the notorious pirate Captain Torrents wrecked the merchant ship. Tumen now sails with the rest of the *Barnacle*'s crew—including Jack—aboard the *Fleur de la Mort*.

Key story:
Jack Sparrow, Vol. 1, *The Coming Storm*

Constance Magliore

First appearance:
Jack Sparrow, Vol 1: *The Coming Storm*

Known relative:
Jean Magliore (brother)

Nicknames:
Rat-Cat-Thingie; Foul Stinky Cat-Thingie; Yucky Beastie Cat-Thing (Jack's favorite); plain old Cat-Thing

Sails aboard:
Barnacle; *Fleur de la Mort*

Weapons and special items:
an incredibly nasty personality

History:
Constance Magliore is the sister of sailor Jean Magliore. According to Jean, Constance was once an ordinary Creole girl. Then the mystic Tia Dalma placed a curse upon her and transformed her into a cat. No one knows why Tia Dalma turned Constance into a feline, and Jean is not telling. But most who know the cat agree that it probably had something to do with her bitter, nasty personality.

Key Stories:
Jack Sparrow, Vol. 1: *The Coming Storm*; Jack Sparrow, Vol. 11: *Poseidon's Peak*

Captain Laura Smith

First appearance:
Jack Sparrow, Vol. 5: *The Age of Bronze*

Known relative:
Arabella Smith (daughter)

Sails aboard:
Fleur de la Mort

History:
The captain of the *Fleur de la Mort* is a force to be reckoned with. Laura Smith left her old life (including her husband and young daughter) at the Faithful Bride to pursue a pirate's life. Laura became a very successful pirate and eventually helmed one of the most prized ships in the Caribbean, the *Fleur de la Mort*. The *Fleur* is fitted with charmed sails; when they are unfurled, the ship becomes invisible to all but those on board. She has an especially close relationship with her first mate, Mr. Reece.

Key story:
Jack Sparrow, Vol. 6, *Silver*.

Captain Torrents

First appearance:
Jack Sparrow, Vol 1: *The Coming Storm*

History:
The feared Captain Torrents was cursed by Davy Jones, and whenever his temper flared up, so did inclement weather. As he was angry rather often, stormy weather followed him wherever he went. He was the first adversary that the crew of the *Barnacle* faced upon taking to the sea. They defeated him by stranding him on an island, but Torrents eventually escaped. When he gained control over his abilities to control the weather, he became a most formidable adversary.

Key stories:
Jack Sparrow, Vol 1: *The Coming Storm*; Jack Sparrow Vol. 12: *Bold New Horizons*

Left-Foot Louis

First appearance:
Jack Sparrow, Vol 3: *The Pirate Chase*

Nickname:
Lefty

Sails aboard:
Cutlass; *Fleur de la Mort* (against his will)

History:
Left-Foot Louis had an ongoing feud with Captain Laura Smith. Arabella, Laura's daughter, believed her mother to have been killed by Louis. Arabella used the power of a mystical weapon known as the Sword of Cortés to inadvertently place Louis aboard Laura's ship, the *Fleur de la Mort*, where he was forced to serve under Captain Smith. In the end, his thirst for power got the best of him, when he joined forces with the nefarious Madame Minuit, who eventually destroyed him.

Key stories:
Jack Sparrow, Vol. 3: *The Pirate Chase*; Jack Sparrow, Vol. 7: *City of Gold*

Madame Minuit

First appearance:
Jack Sparrow, Vol 5: *The Age of Bronze*

Weapons and special abilities:
Madame Minuit is able to summon snakes, which slither down her arms and can hypnotize adversaries. The snakes can also vomit small eggs that can be used for a variety of purposes, including shape-shifting and creating a vanishing screen.

History:
Madame Minuit took control of the city of New Orleans for a time. Using a charmed amulet that was stolen from Tumen's village in the Yucatán, she had the city turned to precious metal and mined. Jack and his crew, on a quest to return the amulet to Tumen's village, defeated the beautiful Madame.

Key stories:
Jack Sparrow, Vol. 5: *The Age of Bronze*; Jack Sparrow, Vol. 7: *City of Gold*

Hernan Cortés

First appearance:
Jack Sparrow, Vol 3: *The Pirate Chase*

Nickname:
Cortsey

History:
Hernan Cortés was the original wielder of the Sword of Cortés. The cursed and all-powerful sword was used by Cortés to slaughter the Aztecs. Hundreds of years later, Jack and his crew were able to locate some clues that led them to the sword, but when Jack obtained it, he got something he hadn't bargained for—the sword's original owner, Hernan Cortés himself, who appeared to oversee the sword and used Jack to do his dirty work. Jack eventually defeated Cortés by calling upon the Heathen Gods and releasing the powerful spirit of Montezuma from captivity.

Key story:
Jack Sparrow, Vol. 4, *The Sword of Cortes*.

The Merfolk

First appearance:
Jack Sparrow, Vol 2: *The Siren Song*

Nickname:
Scaly Tails

History:
"Merfolk" is the name given to the many different races of humanlike sea creatures. The first group of merfolk that Jack Sparrow encountered had the upper bodies of beautiful women—though in one's peripheral vision, they looked grotesque and scaly—and the tails of fish. The ruling class was broken up into three groups: Blue-tails (the leaders), Green-tails (the military arm), and Red-tails (the servants). Eventually, Jack learned that the Blue-tails were controlling the rest of the merfolk population using mystical stones they kept in a hidden chamber they called the Trove. Jack assisted a renegade faction of Purple-tails in overthrowing the only three Blue-tails: Morveren, Aquila, and Aquala. After the revolution, Jack was named ruler of all merfolk, though he delegated day-to-day responsibilities to the Purple-tail Tonra.

Key stories:
Jack Sparrow, Vol. 2: *The Siren Song*; Jack Sparrow, Vol. 4: *The Sword of Cortés*; Jack Sparrow, Vol. 11: *Poseidon's Peak*; Jack Sparrow, Vol. 12: *Bold New Horizons*

And available now . . .

Disney
PIRATES of the CARIBBEAN
LEGENDS OF THE BRETHREN COURT

Volume II:
Rising in the East

Rob Kidd

Based on the earlier adventures of characters created
for the theatrical motion picture,
"Pirates of the Caribbean: The Curse of the Black Pearl"
Screen Story by Ted Elliott & Terry Rossio and
Stuart Beattie and Jay Wolpert,
Screenplay by Ted Elliott & Terry Rossio,
and characters created for the theatrical motion pictures
"Pirates of the Caribbean: Dead Man's Chest" and
"Pirates of the Caribbean: At World's End"
written by Ted Elliott & Terry Rossio

CHAPTER ONE

"**I** knew you didn't have a plan, Jaaaaack!" Hector Barbossa bellowed. "Ye barely even know which end of the ship is up! I bet you've never read a chart in your whole misbegotten, pernicious, confounding—" The rest of his words were (perhaps mercifully) lost in a deluge of water as enormous waves swept over the side of the *Black Pearl*, leaving Barbossa, her first mate, clutching his hat and sputtering.

"What? Eh?" said Captain Jack Sparrow from the helm, cupping his hand around his ear. "Did you hear something?" Jack asked Diego, his kohl-rimmed eyes darting from side to side as if there might be sprites talking in the air all around him. Then he winked at Diego. "Must have been the wind, eh?"

A howling gale raged around the *Black Pearl*, trying with furious force to smash her against the rocks of the Strait of Magellan. Rain lashed the sails and drenched the poor souls on deck, while an icy wind off the South Pole chilled them all to the bone.

The ship had been trapped in what seemed like an endless storm for three days straight as they navigated around the tip of South America, heading for the Pacific Ocean. "Go that way" seemed like a perfectly reasonable plan to Jack. He didn't know what Barbossa was on about— but Barbossa was always grumbling about something, so Jack had learned not to pay much attention.

Diego was too cold to answer Jack. He had never been so cold, not even when he was a young boy sleeping in the stables in the depths of Spain's winter. He wanted to be a good, useful sailor, but his teeth chattered as he clung to the mast and he couldn't feel his fingers or toes anymore. When he saw a slim figure emerge from the hatch, he let go and slid over to her. His shoes slipped and splashed on the soaking deck.

"Carolina!" he yelled over the roar of the storm. "Get back down below! It's too dangerous up here!"

"So why are you out here?" she shouted back. The rain plastered her tunic and trousers to her body instantly despite her long cloak, which was less of a shield and more of a plaything for the wind. Carolina grabbed the edges of the cloak to make sure it didn't fly away, perhaps even taking her with it. "It's just as dangerous for you as it is for me!" she challenged Diego.

"Well—but—but I'm not a princess!" he answered. From the flash of her dark eyes, he knew he'd said the wrong thing.

"I'm not a princess anymore, either!" Carolina snapped, her long dark hair flying wetly around her shoulders. "I'm a pirate now! And if you think I'm just some weak, simpering child of royalty who has to be pampered, I dare you to race me to the bird's nest and we'll just see who's the better sailor!"

Diego felt sick at the thought of climbing the ratlines in this weather. "No, no!" he cried. "That's not what I meant! You're a much better sailor than me! It's not that you're weak—I meant that you're more important than I am!"

The ship heaved to one side, tossing Carolina into Diego's arms as they both stumbled on the slippery deck. He shivered at the nearness of her soft skin and scented hair. "Oh, you are cold," Carolina said, instinctively putting her hands under his shirt to warm him up. He jumped, startled, and to his regret she pulled away, looking embarrassed.

"You have to stop thinking of me as being more important than you," Carolina said, leaning close to him so she didn't have to shout. "We're the same now. Just two pirates aboard Captain Jack Sparrow's ship."

Diego all but ignored her. He tried to stand in a way that would shield Carolina from the bitter wind. The rain lashed against his back.

"Besides," Carolina added, "I couldn't stay below for one more minute. I'd rather be out here in the pouring rain than stuck down there with your 'bonnie lass,' as Captain Sparrow calls her."

"She's not my bonnie lass!" Diego protested. "Stop saying that! She might hear you!"

"Oooooo, *Diego*," Carolina twittered in a perfect imitation of Marcella, the bonnie lass in question. "You're my *hero*, Diego. You're so *smart*, Diego. Take off your *shirt*, Diego."

"Carolina!"

"Oh, calm down," Carolina said with a smile. Neither of them spotted the glimmer of lamplight through the grating over the hatchway below, where another figure was crouched, listening intently. Marcella's eyes narrowed as she drew back further into the shadows. She could only catch a few words through the storm—but she'd heard enough to be sure that Carolina was making fun of her. That Spanish ragamuffin was trying to poison Diego against her! Marcella clenched her fists, wondering if anyone would notice if Carolina "accidentally" fell overboard during the storm. But to do that Marcella would probably have to get wet, and Marcella hated getting wet with a strange, fiery passion. She absolutely refused to go on deck in this weather, no matter who cajoled or entreated her.

"Marcella? What are you doing there?" Jean Magliore, Marcella's cousin, said as he emerged from the crew's quarters, his reddish hair standing up in sleepy tufts.

"Nothing," Marcella snapped. "I don't understand how you can sleep in this horrible boat, with all these horrible smells and all this horrible noise and everything flying around everywhere. I nearly had a barrel fall on me earlier! A whole barrel full of those nasty biscuits they think we're going to eat!"

Jean hid a smile and tried to nod comfortingly.

"And there's no one else down here," Marcella went on, "so you don't have to call me Marcella—which is a stupid name, by the way—"

Jean jumped forward and covered her mouth with his hand. "Shhhh!" he said frantically. He peered around at the flickering shadows belowdecks. "I told you not to talk about that," he whispered. "If Jack finds out who you are, he'll throw us both off the ship, and he won't care if we're in the middle of the Pacific Ocean when he does it!"

Marcella shoved his hand away. "Well, I think that's just rude!" she said.

Just then, Jack flounced by.

"All right, Marcella," Jean said loudly, "why don't we go find out what's for dinner?"

Marcella rolled her eyes and stormed ahead of him toward the galley.

"I *know* what's for dinner," she sniped at top volume. "Something *truly horrible* with a side of something very nasty, plus a 'biscuit' with all the flavor and texture of a New Orleans cobblestone."

Jean glanced around nervously one more time and then followed her. He tried not to look straight at any of the hanging lanterns, which were swinging madly as the ship bounced over the waves. Marcella was one of the few who had not been affected at all by seasickness during this storm. Somehow she was still able to eat astonishing amounts of food, complaining vigorously over every bite.

Unfortunately for the rest of the crew, Marcella did have a point. The situation in the galley had deteriorated rapidly after the *Pearl*'s cook, Gombo, had gone off to captain his own pirate ship as Gentleman Jocard. While the *Pearl* had been sailing south along the coast of Argentina, the pirates had gone ashore several times for fruit, but now it had been days since their last landfall, and the remaining food supplies did not look very appetizing.

Billy Turner was sitting at the long table in the galley with his head in his hands. Jack had lured him onto the *Black Pearl* with the promise that he would take Billy straight back to his family in North Carolina. But Billy should have known better than to believe anything Jack said. Now he was trapped on this mad expedition to

Asia, with no prospect of getting home anytime soon.

After a brief encounter with the creepiest mystic in the Caribbean, Tia Dalma, Jack was on a mission to collect vials of Shadow Gold to defeat the Shadow Lord and his Shadow Army,* whatever that was all about, and Billy was fairly certain he was stuck on this ship at least until the Shadow Gold was found. At *least*.

The vials of Shadow Gold Jack was looking for had been scattered by Tia Dalma's zombie, Alex, and they were now being held by five of the nine Pirate Lords around the world. The problem was figuring out *which* Pirate Lords had them. Jack had run into the Spanish Pirate Lord, Villanueva, while Jack was liberating a wayward vial from the Incas. So now Jack knew two things: Villanueva did not have a vial. And, according to the rumors, Mistress Ching— Pirate Lord of the Pacific Ocean, based in China—did. That was enough for Jack.

* As detailed in Vol. 1, *The Caribbean.*

"Cheer up, Billy," Jean said, clapping him on the shoulder. "Just think, we're going to Asia! We're going to see Shanghai and Hong Kong and Singapore again—and who knows what else!"

"I *know* what else," Billy said gloomily. "Lots of water. Lots of angry pirates. Lots of swords in our faces. It won't be any different than the last time we were there."

"Why, you don't think Mistress Ching will just hand over her vial of Shadow Gold?" Jean said with a cheerful grin. "Jack is *très bon* at persuasion, after all."

Billy snorted. "Perchance you're forgetting the last few times Jack has tried to charm somebody into doing what he wants."

"He charmed you onto this ship, didn't he, *mon ami*?" Jean winked.

Billy grimaced.

"I'm not eating *this*," Marcella interrupted, slamming a hardtack biscuit down on the table. The biscuits were round and sturdy and could last for months. They were baked ahead of time exactly for a trip like this. In fact, as far as Jean could tell, these biscuits already had lasted for months. Possibly years. Maybe . . . centuries?

Marcella repeatedly banged the biscuit against the side of the table. It went CLONK, CLONK, CLONK, like a hammer against a nail. Not even a crumb fell off. The biscuits were called "hardtack" for a reason.

"I'm not breaking my perfect teeth on something this horrible," Marcella said. ("Perfect" was a bit of a stretch, Billy thought. In truth, Marcella's teeth were a bit yellow, a bit crooked, and surprisingly small.) "And I'm not eating *that*, whatever it is," she went on, pointing to a barrel of dried salt pork that looked orange and wrinkled and flaky. "And I'm definitely not eating *these* nasty things." She ran her fingers through a barrel of shriveled brown peas and shuddered.

"You miss Gombo, don't you?" Jean said.

"I most certainly do not," Marcella said, throwing her shoulders back and crossing her arms. "That ungrateful, self-centered wretch just sailed away without even a good-bye. Leaving us with no cook at all! He didn't spend even one second thinking of what would happen to the rest of us! He's just a stupid, dreadful *pirate*. I don't care if I never see him again!" She tossed her stringy hair.

Jean looked at her closely. Were those . . . tears in her eyes?

BOOM!

A muffled sound, like faraway thunder, echoed through the ship. Jean and Billy exchanged worried glances. Surely that wasn't—

BOOM!

The ship rocked as if something heavy had just landed in the water beside it.

Something like a cannonball.

"Anyway, he never cooked my fish as rare as I like it, and he was all big and muscley and— hey!" Marcella realized that Billy and Jean had raced away to the deck. "I was *talking*, people!" she fumed. "Pirates!" She threw the biscuit at the wall. It bounced off and hit the floor with a dull, unappetizing thud.

Jean poked his head through the hatch and realized that the storm was finally dying down. The heavy rain had become a light shower, tapping gently on the boards of the deck. The cold wind still whistled through the black sails, but something much more urgent than the thunderstorm had appeared on the horizon.

Two ships were bearing down on the *Black Pearl* with frightening speed. It was as if they had hidden behind the thunderclouds, lying in wait until the *Pearl* reached the end of the strait and came upon the open waters of the Pacific Ocean.

Even through the rain, Jack recognized the winglike shape of the red sails, the sleek outline of the ships, and the bright crimson banners fluttering from the masts. He snapped his spyglass shut. These were Chinese pirate junks, a class of ship known throughout the world for its speed and maneuverability. But here? At the gateway to the Pacific, just off the South American coast? It was clear that someone did not want the *Pearl* to enter the Pacific Ocean, and Jack had a good idea who that might be.

If there were ever a time for the *Pearl*'s legendary swiftness to be tested, this was it! But first they had to get around the junks, which were planted directly in their path.

The adventure continues in the swashbuckling series
Legends of the Brethren Court
available now wherever books are sold!